Ghost Cat

Ghost Cat

by HELEN RUSHMORE

Illustrated by Reisie Lonette

Cover by Carol Wilde

SCHOLASTIC BOOK SERVICES

NEW YORK • TORONTO • LONDON • AUCKLAND • SYDNEY

1st printing . . . . March 1971
Printed in the U. S. A.

To Olive, my sister

Contents

Ghost Cat

1

At the Haunted House

No. I won't go," said Len stubbornly. "And you're crazy if you go."

He pushed his hands into his overall pockets and leaned against the big oak tree. Glory could tell by the tight look around his mouth that there was no use pleading with him.

"All right, Mr. Len. If you're afraid I'll go by myself."

She turned to run but Len caught her by her short uptilted braids.

3

"Not so fast," he said good-naturedly. "Not so fast. How do you know Mamma will let you?"

He held the yellow braids tightly and grinned exasperatingly as Glory squirmed and twisted to get away.

"Let go," she said. "Mamma won't care. She'll be glad that she's got one child that's not afraid of ghosts. Turn me loose. I'm going."

Len opened his hand and Glory whirled away from him. She ran along the path that led down Wolf Hill. Len took two or three slow steps after her and then he stopped. Glory didn't look back. He whistled shrilly but she ran on. He sat down and leaned against the tree, his eyes still on the path down which Glory had disappeared. Reaching into his pocket he felt among nails, string, fish hooks, a rabbit foot, and a buckeye and found his knife. He opened the blade and began to sharpen it on a sandstone. He halfway wished he'd gone with Glory.

Glory was still angry as she ran down the hill and splashed across Deer Creek. The water splattered over her clean starched dress but she didn't care. She had more important things on her mind than clean dresses.

On the other side of the creek the path divided.

4

Glory took the left-hand path which led around Deer Knob. Usually she took the right one that led to Granny Baker's cabin halfway up Deer Knob. Now she only glanced that way and wondered what Granny would say if she knew Glory was on her way alone to the haunted house in Happy Hollow.

Glory slowed down to a walk but she couldn't stop to rest. The old folks said Miss Nancy's ghost walked only at sunset. Glory wanted to see the ghost —if the story were true.

She didn't believe the ghost would come but Len thought it would. Sometimes Len was downright foolish about all those ghost stories. Even if he was her brother and twelve years old he didn't have much spunk when it came to dark graveyards and old cabins where everyone who had lived in them was dead and gone. He wouldn't go near a place if he'd even once heard a scary story about it.

Like Witch Cave right at the foot of their own hill. Glory had begged him all summer to take her into the cave. But no. All because the old folks told a lot of silly granny-tales about it.

Mamma and Papa both had told him there were no ghosts but some of the old folks said there were. Between them Len didn't know what to believe. If he was ever to take her into Witch Cave, Glory now had to prove to him there was no ghost at Happy Hollow.

She glanced at the sun. The time was growing short if she was to reach the haunted house by sunset. The winding path swung away from the trees and joined a dusty road. Glory began to run again.

It was not far now and she had the road to herself. Long ago it had been a busy highway, Papa said. She would be lucky this afternoon if she saw a boy on horseback or a wandering cow switch the dust from the goldenrod by the wayside. The road curved lazily around the hill and dipped into the valley.

There it lay—the haunted house of Happy Hollow. Glory had forgotten how deserted the place was. How desolate and lonely the old house looked with its row of upstairs windows blank with broken panes. The door, loose upon its hinges, stood wide open. Almost like an invitation to enter, Glory thought. But she knew that few people would walk through that open door.

She stopped by the stone pillars that still proudly marked the gateway to the Rose Plantation. The once well-kept lawn was overgrown with weeds and brambles. Dead branches from the huge shade trees littered the yard and were themselves half hidden by wild blackberry bushes.

The lilac bushes by the chimney had grown roof high. In the spring they were white with blossoms and the sweet scent of them filled Happy Hollow. A rosebush, left to run at will through the long years, completely filled one corner of the yard.

"Like the thorn hedge around the Sleeping Beauty's Castle," Glory thought as she started up the path.

She crossed the smooth flagstones that formed the floor of the porch. She peered through the door. The room was empty now except for dried leaves which had swirled in through the broken window panes and acorns, probably carried in by the birds and squirrels.

Her bare feet made no noise yet Glory tiptoed as she crossed the room. She felt as if she shouldn't be here. As if she were intruding on the privacy of strangers.

The wealthy Rose family weren't exactly strangers even though they had lived and died so many years ago. Everyone in the mountains knew their story. The legend of the beautiful Nancy Rose was as fa-

7

miliar to Glory as the story of Cinderella and much more real.

Many a night while the fire burned low she had listened to Granny Baker tell of the willful headstrong girl whose mother had died when the little one was barely able to walk. How the baby, brought up by servants, grew to be a beautiful woman, spoiled and pampered by her father.

Everyone knew how the young and handsome Thomas Miles was forbidden to the plantation all because he was poor. How Nancy had quarreled with her father and threatened to run away with Thomas. Then one evening just at sunset when Thomas rode up to the door, a shot rang out from the nearby woods. And Nancy, her arms filled with white lilacs, had found him dead upon the flagstones.

It was never proved that Mr. Rose had fired the shot but the story was that Nancy never spoke to her father again. Before the lilacs had finished their blooming Nancy Rose was dead. Soon Mr. Rose died, too, alone and brokenhearted.

The emptiness of the house, the small scuffling of the leaves in the wind, frightened Glory. She backed swiftly from the room. It was better out of doors where she could see the birds and perhaps hear a dog bark.

Curling her feet under her she sat down on the flagstones and leaned against one of the pillars that supported the sagging roof of the porch. The sun was almost ready to drop behind the mountain. It was time for the ghost of Miss Nancy to appear from behind the lilac bushes—beautiful Miss Nancy, dressed all in white, her golden hair tied with a blue ribbon and her arms full of sweet-smelling flowers.

Glory waited, her heart beating wildly in her throat. She didn't believe in the ghost but lots of folks did. They said they had seen her close enough to touch her white arms. They said they had seen the sparkle of her rings and had smelled the lilacs even though it was autumn when the leaves were red. Len believed too and he was two whole years older than Glory.

"I don't believe," she whispered. "I don't believe."

Glory's eyes shifted from the lilac bushes swaying gently in the evening breeze to the golden ball of the sun dropping quickly behind the mountain. Now only the golden rim was left. Now—it was gone.

Glory held her breath and waited but no little ghost of Miss Nancy appeared. There were only the

lilacs, the waving grass and the clear call of a meadow lark. Glory knew it wouldn't happen. It couldn't happen. There was no such thing as a ghost. And yet—folks said she was so beautiful.

Glory stood up. She took a deep breath and rubbed the tingly prickly feeling from her hands and feet. Out of the corner of her eye she saw something move beside the lilac bush. Something small and white. She heard a low cry. Glory stared, half frightened, unable to believe her eyes.

Picking her way across the grass, her long fluffy tail lifted high like a banner, came a cat. At least Glory thought it was a cat. She hoped it was a cat. But she had never seen one like this before.

She was white. White as spring lilacs and her hair was long. Soft to touch, Glory was sure. Her eyes were blue and around her neck was a narrow blue ribbon. Once it must have been a bow but now the ribbon was bedraggled and dirty and the little cat tripped on it as she walked.

The cat rubbed against Glory's bare leg and Glory jumped, bumping her head against the stone pillar. Was it a cat or wasn't it. It simply couldn't be real. Glory had waited for Miss Nancy's ghost with her white dress, her blue ribbon and her proud blue eyes. Instead came this tiny creature with white fur, torn blue ribbon and pleading blue eyes.

The cat looked up and meowed, a faint little meow, and Glory laughed aloud. This was no ghost cry. It said plainly enough that she was a real cat and she was hungry.

Then to Glory's astonishment the little cat sat up. She lifted her right paw to the side of her face in a soldier-like salute and meowed again. Glory dropped to her knees and put her arms around the thin little body. The cat snuggled her head under Glory's chin and lay still. She meowed once more as if to say, "Let's go."

"All right, Miss Nancy Rose." Glory laughed as the name slipped from her lips. "We'll go but you won't be welcomed by anyone but me."

2

Bad Luck Cat

THE HOLLOWS were filled with dusky shadows as Glory climbed Wolf Hill, the cat cuddled close in her arms. She walked slowly, putting off as long as possible the moment when she must face Mamma and Papa and Len.

If it were only a dog she was bringing home there would be no trouble. The whole Moore family would scurry around to make the lost creature comfortable. They would find some clean gunny sacks to make a bed. They would fill a dish with table scraps. They would pump cool water for him to drink.

But stray cats were something else. Stray cats brought bad luck. It was bad luck to move a cat too. Glory wondered if Miss Nancy Rose had been left on the doorstep of some empty house. Had she waited and waited for someone to call her in? To give her warm milk? To pet her? Had she finally wandered off to hunt her food in the woods, alone and unwanted until Glory found her?

Glory sat down on a log and began to pick out the burs and sticks that had caught in the long hair. She smoothed out the ragged ribbon and tied it again around Miss Nancy Rose's neck. The cat drew a long breath and stretched out her legs. Glory sat for a time, running her fingers through the long fur and looking up the hill toward home.

It wasn't only that Mamma thought stray cats brought bad luck. Mamma didn't really like cats. She called them sly suspicious creatures. Always slinking around barns. Wandering away from home every moonlit night. Stealing cream from the spring-house once the door was left open the tiniest crack. Cats were just a nuisance and a trouble as far as

Mamma was concerned. Len didn't like cats either and Papa would do what Mamma said.

Glory thought about the twins. They might like Miss Nancy Rose. Even though they were only five they could be a big help. Honey and Cubby were noisy and persistent once they set their hearts on something. Maybe they would set their hearts on Miss Nancy Rose.

Mamma was standing on the porch looking down the path as Glory walked across the yard. Papa was already in from the field and was resting on the steps. The twins tumbled about his feet. Glory could hear Len whistling in the barn as he milked the cow. She was later than she thought.

"You're late, child," said Mamma gravely. "Len said you went to Happy Hollow on some wild goose chase."

"Yes, I went to Happy Hollow," Glory said. She didn't know how to go on. Miss Nancy Rose was asleep and Mamma hadn't noticed her. "I—I—found something down there."

The twins rushed up to her.

"What'd you find, Glory?" shouted Cubby.

"Let me see," cried Honey. "I want to see."

"Not Miss Nancy's ghost," exclaimed Mamma. "That I can't believe."

"No. Not exactly," said Glory, trying to laugh. "I named her Miss Nancy Rose but she's not a ghost. She's a—a cat."

"A cat," said Mamma impatiently. "Of all things. Glory Moore, you know better than to bring a stray cat home. Take her outside the gate and put her down. A stray cat! Mercy to goodness!"

Glory held the cat closer and looked pleadingly at her mother.

"Look at her, Mamma, before you say no," she said.

"I don't need to look at her to know that I don't want her around." Mamma turned toward the kitchen door. "I'll have no stray cats bringing bad luck to this house."

"Please, Mamma," begged Glory. "Only look. Just once. You've never seen a cat like this before."

"Now, Glory," Mamma began. "I said no and I mean—"

"Oh, the sweet little kitty," cried Honey, holding out her arms. "I want to hold her."

Honey sat down on the porch and Glory put the cat into her lap.

17

"She needs a haircut," said Cubby, running his fingers through her thick ruff.

"She is kind of pretty," Papa said.

Mamma's curiosity overcame her ill feelings and she turned to look.

"Where did you get her, Glory?" asked Papa.

"Where'd you get what?" demanded Len as he put the milk pail on the porch and peered over Cubby's red head.

"Down at the haunted house," answered Glory. "She was hiding in the lilac bushes."

"In the lilac bushes," exclaimed Len uneasily. "Miss Nancy's ghost is supposed to come from the lilac bushes. This cat is just like the ghost. White dress, blue ribbon, blue eyes. For the love of Pete, Glory, you've brought home a ghost cat."

"Don't be such a dope," said Glory in disgust. "You know she's a real cat."

"That will do, Len," said Papa firmly. "We'll have no more talk about ghost cats. But, Glory, Mamma is right. We don't want any stray cats. Put her over the fence."

"She's half starved," pleaded Glory. "Can't I feed her just this once?"

"Feed her once and you'll have her on the doorstep the rest of her life," replied Papa.

To have the cat on her doorstep was exactly what Glory wanted but she knew better than to argue. She took the cat from Honey's lap and held her close. Miss Nancy Rose lifted her paws to Glory's neck and tucked her head under Glory's chin. Nervous chills swept through her body and Glory could feel the wildly thumping heart through the thick fur.

"Poor little cat," she said sadly. "You've got no home. You're starving to death and we've got buckets and buckets of milk."

Tears rolled out of Honey's eyes, Cubby sniffled and Papa looked decidedly uncomfortable.

"Besides all of that," Glory went on, "the only one who loves you is going to have to throw you over the fence."

Honey sobbed bitterly.

"Papa. Papa," she begged, throwing her arms about her father's neck. "Don't make Glory throw her away. Maybe I'll be lost some day. What if a big old man threw me over the fence without a bite to eat or a little bitty drink of m-i-lk."

Papa patted Honey's head and glanced helplessly at Mamma.

"Well—ah—she seems harmless enough. Ah—uh—what do you say, Mamma?"

"What is there to say?" Mamma asked disapprovingly. "The cat stays. Give her some milk, Glory. But mind, she can't come into the house."

Honey snatched the cat from Glory's arms. Before anyone could stop her she had poked the cat's head into the pail of milk. The cat, spitting and choking, clawed desperately at the tin pail.

"There, there, my little kitty," said Honey soothingly. "Drink some milk."

"Not that way," shouted Papa.

He scooped up the cat and wiped her off with his bandana handkerchief. Then he handed her back to Glory.

"You young ones let her alone until Glory teaches you how to take care of her."

Honey looked abashed.

"I'm sorry. I didn't mean to hurt her," she apologized, putting her hands behind her and stepping back out of the way.

Her heels struck the milk pail. The next instant Honey's blue overalled legs waved wildly in the air and her fat little backside was stuck fast in the bucket. Honey, milk and the bucket splashed and clattered down the steps.

"The bad luck's started," cried Len.

He grabbed Honey's arms while Cubby tugged manfully at the bucket.

"Papa! Mamma! Everybody help," yelled Cubby. "I can't get it off. She's stuck for good and always."

The thought of wearing the big bucket for good and always on the most inconvenient place possible changed Honey's angry howls to wails of terror. Papa dashed to the rescue. He lifted Honey and Len pulled at the bucket. She slipped out with a sucking gurgling sound. Cubby breathed an immense sigh of relief.

"She sounds just like a cow taking her foot out of the mud," he said.

3

More Bad Luck

GLORY OPENED her eyes and yawned. The early morning sun streamed across the patchwork quilt flung over the foot of the bed. The ruffled curtains swung lazily in the breeze. Glory stretched and wondered why she felt so happy. Something pleasant must have happened but being only half awake she couldn't for the moment remember what it was.

She looked at the twins asleep in the big bed on the other side of the room. Except for their hair they were remarkably alike. Even in sleep Honey's yellow hair lay smooth—not at all like Cubby's which always looked as if he had crawled out of a brush heap backward.

Poor Honey. Glory wondered if she would always be jealous of Cubby's red curls. And Cubby—proud as a peacock because his tousled mop looked exactly like Papa's. The twins' eyes popped open almost at the same instant.

"Where's the cat, Glory?" called Cubby as he tumbled out of bed and grabbed his overalls.

"Mercy me! I almost forgot." Glory reached for her clothes. "I'll race you."

Cubby struggled into his overalls and gave a gasp of dismay.

"Glory," he said solemnly, "which is the baddest luck? To change your clothes back when you get 'em on wrong or to walk backwards all day?"

"In your case, I should think to walk backwards all day," replied Glory, smiling at his twisted overalls.

By the time she had them turned about and fastened, Honey was in the kitchen. Glory could hear her talking to Miss Nancy Rose. The little cat, her pink nose pressed against the screen, waited expect-

24

antly. Her plumy tail waved excitedly as Glory hurried to her.

"Glory, you've got to get rid of that cat."

Glory stopped, her hand already on the door, and looked at Papa. Something terrible must have happened to make him sound like that. The dread and fear of yesterday rushed over her again.

"What happened?" she asked uneasily. "What did she do?"

"She killed three baby chicks last night."

Glory stared at the cat in puzzled disbelief. Slow tears gathered in her eyes.

"She's a chicken-killer," continued Papa. "You know what that means."

A chicken-killer. Glory knew there was no place on a farm for a cat that killed chickens. But how did Papa know that it was Miss Nancy Rose who had killed the chicks? And if she had, she killed only because she was hungry.

"I can teach her to let them alone." Glory looked pleadingly at her father. "She's been used to hunting her own food. She still thinks she has to. Let me teach her."

"Once a killer, always a killer," replied Papa firmly.

"But you aren't sure, are you?"

"There's no use talking. Stray cats are no-good varmints. Bad luck and trouble follow them."

There was a note of finality in Papa's voice which kept Glory from saying anything more but it was hard to believe that Miss Nancy Rose was bad. There must be some mistake. She looked at the cat whose strange blue eyes had become anxious and questioning.

Miss Nancy Rose seemed to sense that something was wrong. There was a disconsolate droop to her tail as she studied Glory's troubled face. Her long whiskers and sensitive nose twitched inquiringly in her effort to understand Glory's unhappiness. Suddenly she made her decision. With a determined air she trotted down the steps and disappeared into the barn.

"She said she didn't kill the old chickens," said Honey. "Didn't she, Cubby?"

"Yes, she did," agreed Cubby. "But what's so bad if she did? Mamma kills them when they're big and we eat them."

"Papa likes lots of fried chicken," Honey pointed out.

Papa walked to the window and with his hands

deep in his pockets, he watched the white mist rise from the mountains. It rose in plumy streaks, peculiarly like the fluffy tail of a cat. There was a strained silence as Mamma rolled and cut the biscuits and Glory stumbled about setting the table for breakfast.

The biscuits were browned and Mamma was pouring Papa's coffee when the tension was broken by a loud throaty song of triumph. Miss Nancy Rose, her claws hooked in the wire, savagely battered the screen door and demanded entrance.

Cubby hastily swung the door open and Miss Nancy Rose marched in, a huge gray rat dangling from her mouth. She laid it proudly at Glory's feet.

The twins tore around the room, screaming and kicking as if the rat were already gnawing at their ankles. Mamma grabbed her skirts and leaped upon a chair, the coffee pot showering its scalding contents on anyone and everyone who was in its way as it shot across the room and came to rest, upside down in the corner.

Glory reached for the broom and popped it down on the still wriggling rat. Papa rolled it in a paper and carried it out of doors.

"See," said Cubby when Papa was back and the excitement had died down. "It wasn't Miss Nancy

Rose that killed the chickens. It was that old ratter rob— I mean robber rat."

Papa, relieved at the unexpected turn the situation had taken, smiled at Mamma.

"I think you are right, Cubby," he said. "I'm sure it was the ratter rob."

"What's a ratter rob?" demanded Honey. "Is that rat talk?"

"Within reason it was the rat," agreed Mamma. "Glory, take the pitcher and pour your cat some cream."

"Have I missed something?" Len yawned noisily and, still half asleep, dragged himself to the wash basin on the porch. "For Pete's sake! Is that pesky cat here?"

"She's not a pesky cat," said Honey. "She caught a rat."

"What's so wonderful about that?" said Len, indifferently. "It was probably a little bitty old mouse."

"It was too a rat, wasn't it, Cubby?"

Cubby, stretched flat on his stomach to watch the steady stream of cream flow upward into Miss Nancy Rose's mouth, looked scornfully at Len's sleepy face.

"Yes, she did," he answered. "And besides that she's perlite. She washes her face."

"Shucks," Len said peevishly as he flipped cold water on Glory for her provoking laugh. "What are we going to do today?" he asked by way of changing the subject.

"Pick blackberries for Granny Baker," replied Glory. "Don't you remember?"

"Oh, yes." Len looked around to see where his father was. "That sorry old ghost cat of yours made me forget. She's probably cast a spell over my mind."

29

"Your what?" asked Glory.

But Len chose to ignore that remark. He looked across the valley to Deer Knob where a thin column of rising smoke was faintly pink in the early morning sun. Granny wasn't their real grandmother but they loved her as if she were. Everyone for miles around loved Granny Baker. Come sickness or trouble, Granny was there with her herb medicines and her warm sympathy. But being Granny's nearest neighbors the Moore family felt as if she really belonged to them.

"Len," called Mamma. "This breakfast's ruined. You'll have time to milk before I can fix another."

"Ho-hum." Len yawned again and dashed several drops of cold water on his face. He shuddered and fumbled for the towel.

"Cubby," he said brightly. "Someday I'm going to teach you to milk. Won't that be fun?"

"Nope," replied Cubby. "It's funner to watch you milk."

"Wouldn't you even get the bucket for me?"

"Nope. The bucket's too big. I'm a little bitty boy. And Honey's too little too," he added quickly.

The twins grinned at each other and settled themselves more firmly on the steps.

"That kid's too smart," Len muttered to Glory as he walked over to the peach tree and reached for the bucket where it hung in the sun. "When I was his age I fell for sweet talk like that. Look where it got me. On the milking end of a cow."

He found the bucket and went whistling to the barn. Miss Nancy Rose left off cleaning her whiskers and scampered after him. The twins scampered after Miss Nancy Rose.

They were gone so long that Mamma didn't wait breakfast for them. Papa had finished when they came up the path with Miss Nancy Rose riding on Len's shoulder.

"She's not so bad after all," Len said, lifting her down and giving her head a soothing pat. "She can sit up and catch milk in her mouth."

"You don't say," exclaimed Papa. "How did you teach her?"

"I was kind of provoked when she followed me," explained Len with a sidelong glance at Glory. "I thought I'd scare her with a squirt of milk. First she tried to catch it with her paws and the milk splashed all over her face. Once she got a taste of it, she sat up with her mouth open and all I had to do was aim right."

31

While the rest of the family gazed in admiration at Glory's smart cat, Honey climbed into her chair and helped herself to biscuits and jam.

"Oh, Honey," said Mamma, catching sight of her dirty face. "You haven't washed. Even Miss Nancy Rose washes her face."

"Not before she eats," Honey mumbled through a mouthful of biscuit.

"That's right," said Cubby. "That way she only has to wash once."

Papa hastily pushed back his chair and left the room.

4

Witch Cave

GLORY LOOKED at her heaping bucket with satisfaction. If there was anything prettier than ripe berries she didn't know what it was. Each one shining like a jewel and smelling better than perfume. Granny Baker would be proud of them. Glory wondered if Len's bucket was as full as hers.

They had been picking since early afternoon and now she was tired. She looked around for Len but she couldn't see him anywhere. But then—he was probably on the other side of the path just as far away from Witch Cave as he could get. But for her—the closer the better.

She set her bucket down carefully so as not to spill the berries. Then she picked her way along the rocks until she reached the edge of the cliff. Stretching out on her stomach she peered over the ledge.

A little shiver of excitement ran down her spine. There it lay, just as she had seen it hundreds of times—Witch Hollow, shadowy and cool, with Deer Creek circling into a wide still pool and Witch Cave black against the rocks. No matter how many times she came upon the place she always felt a little chill which set her scalp to tingling.

She wasn't afraid. It was just that there were so many stories about Witch Cave. Good scary stories that she loved but which frightened the living daylights out of Len.

Grandpappy Bundie's story was the best. More than once she had listened to him tell how, when he was young, he had seen a ghost float out of Witch Cave and disappear over the tops of the trees in Witch Hollow. It was wailing and carrying on something terrible—so he said.

Never since that night had Grandpappy Bundie gone to Witch Hollow alone. Not even the time his pack of hounds treed a possum there. He let them rave and bark all night long—so he said. Along toward daybreak a storm came up and those dogs streaked home a-yiping to wake the dead. When he opened the door to see what the ruckus was about the whole pack was trembling like the leaves on the aspen trees.

Glory wanted to see the ghost that had frightened Grandpappy—if it were true. She wanted to see it sail out over Witch Hollow even if it made her shake like the leaves on an aspen tree. She couldn't say anything to Grandpappy Bundie but privately she had her doubts about the whole story.

She heard Len's pail clatter against the rocks. He came over and sat beside her.

"Is your bucket full?" she asked without turning around to look.

"Yep."

Nothing more was said for a time. Each was gazing at the black hole of Witch Cave.

"Len." Glory broke the silence first. "Will you—?"

"No, I won't."

"Why?"

"You know why."

"That's no sensible reason."

"I don't care."

Glory knew there was no use to go on teasing. He was a strange boy, believing in lucky stones and buckeyes and all sorts of charm words and rhymes.

There was no sense in a boy as nice as Len being so foolish. He wasn't afraid of anything except ghosts and haunted places. Glory couldn't believe he was really afraid of them. Only he went to a lot of trouble if he wasn't, fetching home all the horseshoes he found, picking up every white button and leaving the black ones lie.

In other ways he was brave. Glory remembered the time Bud Miller threw a snake on her at school. Bud was fourteen, and half a head taller than Len, but Bud lost a tooth that day. Minnie Miller skipped arithmetic class to find spider webs to put on the cuts so as to stop the bleeding.

Len fumbled around in his pocket and pulled out a big apple.

"Do you want half?" he asked, opening his knife, and Glory nodded.

"Wait." Glory took the knife and sniffed along the blade. Sometimes Len's knife smelled like rabbit fur or fish scales or worse. "It's all right," she said, handing it back to him. "You can use it."

"Some folks are too particular for their own good," Len grumbled.

He cut the apple, measured the pieces and with a sidelong glance, he handed her the smallest.

"Piggy," she said, laughing at the size of her piece. "I thought you said half."

"I'm the man." Len gave her a smug, satisfied grin. "I ought to have the biggest."

"Then why don't you take me into the cave?"

Len suddenly became very busy counting the seeds in his apple core. He spread them along his hand, then pressed the seeds to his forehead.

"How many stuck?" he asked.

"Three," said Glory. "What did you wish?"

"I wished that you'd keep still about Witch Cave," he replied glumly. "But I've got to wait three days before it will come true. Three more days of your nagging. Do you know what they did to women in the olden days when they nagged their menfolks?"

"No. What?"

"They ducked them in the pond." Len shook his finger at Glory. "It wasn't such a bad idea to my way of thinking."

"Deer Creek isn't deep enough for you to duck me except right in front of the cave." Glory looked up hopefully. "That's an idea. The deep part is right in front of it."

Len turned his back on her and tossed an acorn at a squirrel on a branch above his head.

"Oh, dear," said Glory disconsolately. "Nothing ever happens in these mountains."

Len looked all around, almost as if he were seeing the hills for the first time. The distant mountains were wrapped in mist—mist so blue and high that it became part of the sky. Below, wave after wave of hills stretched on to meet the blue. Green hills, green of cedar and pine, green of hickory and dogwood and oak. The green of the Ozark Mountains rolling on and on until it became the blue of the rim of the sky.

"They're mighty pretty hills, though," said Len thoughtfully. "Look at them changing color with every cloud that passes overhead. A body shouldn't need a sight like that and excitement too."

"I do," Glory said positively. "I want to go into Witch Cave."

"Glory June Moore!" Len jumped up and grabbed his bucket. "You're like an old snapping turtle. Once you get hold of an idea you don't let go 'til it thunders."

Glory picked up her bucket and followed him.

"All signs point to a dry spell," she said with a giggle. "Thunder is a long way off. Don't forget those apple seeds. I've got three days before you duck me."

5

Len Makes a Promise

GLORY LOOKED around the kitchen before she turned down the light. The supper dishes were washed and the table set for breakfast. Everything was neat and in order—everything, that is, except the floor. Folks didn't sweep the dirt out of doors after dark.

She stepped to the porch to look for Miss Nancy Rose. She called but no cat appeared. She's probably out hunting, Glory decided as she went through the house and joined the rest of the family on the front porch.

The night was cool and pleasant. A new moon hung high above the trees. A wet moon, too, with one point higher than the other. That was good. The garden needed rain. It was good too that Glory's first glimpse of the moon was after it was high in the sky. Seeing a new moon through the branches of trees was the worst kind of bad luck.

Settling herself comfortably against the post Glory listened to the night sounds. Whippoorwills called off in the hollows, making the dark lonely with their pleading songs. Lightning bugs sparkled like diamond rings. Summer nights were pleasant here in the hills.

Away off Glory could hear dogs baying at some treed animal. That wasn't so pleasant. She was sorry for the little animal looking down on a pack of leaping howling dogs, seeing their big tushes and dripping tongues, feeling their hot breath. She hoped they weren't barking at Miss Nancy Rose. But she put that thought out of her mind. Miss Nancy Rose was too smart to let herself be caught by a pack of dogs.

Glory looked at the twins half asleep on Papa's lap. Papa was singing *A Frog He Would A-Wooing Go,* tapping his heels in time to the music. Mamma

swayed slowly back and forth in her rocking chair. One rocker creaked with every backward swing.

"There now," exclaimed Papa, breaking off in the middle of his song. "I mighty near forgot. Charley Curtis passed the word along that Granny Baker has finished with some rugs and wants Len to carry them down to the gift shop."

"I'll be proud to." Len spoke up quickly. "When? Tomorrow?"

"I'll need your help in the morning," answered Papa. "The signs point to rain and I want to get the hay in. Get the rugs after dinner."

That suited Glory. A whole afternoon off. They could take Granny the berries, pick up her rugs and come back by Witch Cave. If only Len would go.

"Papa," she asked. "Did you ever go into Witch Cave?"

"A long time ago when I was a young one," he replied. "Why?"

"I want to go," said Glory. "Are the stories true that folks tell about it? The ones about haunts and ghosts?"

"It don't stand to reason they are," Papa answered.

He begin to sing again but Glory wasn't through. "What did Grandpappy Bundie see that made him think it was a ghost?"

"Probably mist rising from the water," he answered. "All that happened when he was a young man. He's over ninety years old now. A man is liable to forget after all those years. Especially if his mind is set on believing something different."

"He said he heard something too," continued Glory.

"I know," Papa replied. "There are others who say they've heard things too. I've never been lucky enough to be down there at the right time."

"Lucky!" exclaimed Len. "What would be lucky about that?"

Papa laughed at Len's horrified gasp.

"There's always some reasonable explanation for those things if folks search long enough," he said. "My grandpa was the man who could tell tales about the cave but they weren't ghost stories."

Len and Glory moved up closer so as not to miss anything. Mamma stopped rocking and drew up her chair.

"It wasn't long after Grandpa staked his claim on this land that he began to see curious lights and white figures and to hear strange noises. Not being the kind that scared easily he went down to investigate. A bullet took the tail off his coonskin cap. Grandpa admired that cap and he was considerably annoyed when the tail went sailing through the air.

"He gathered together a few homesteaders and went down to the cave one evening just about dusk. Two men were sitting by a fire eating supper.

45

Grandpa and the men closed in on them and asked them what their business might be. They said they were hunting gold that the Spaniards had hidden in the cave. They said they had a map showing this to be one of the old treasure caves.

"Some of the homesteaders were inclined to believe them but Grandpa was riled up on account of the tail of his cap. He told his friends to keep their guns right steady on the two and he'd hunt a little Spanish gold himself.

"He went in and found gold all right but it was gold from a train robbery that had taken place about a month before. They turned the men over to the marshal. Grandpa had had the foresight to include him in the search party. They found a couple of sheets in the corner of the cave. The men confessed they used them to wrap up in when they left the cave. Anyone seeing them would think the place was haunted and stay away."

"Probably that's where a lot of those stories got started," said Mamma. "And a lot of addlepated folks carried them on."

"Is it really an old Spanish treasure cave?" asked Len.

"Well, there wasn't any map," replied Papa. "Grandpa did a good job of cleaning out the place too."

"Did you ever find anything that might prove it was a Spanish cave?" asked Glory.

"Nothing much. Grandpa found an old sword with a broken blade. He didn't rightly know whether it was a Spanish sword or not. It could have been from the French traders or an Indian could have brought it into this part of the country."

"What happened to it?" asked Len. "I'd sure like to see it."

"It kicked around the house when I was a young one about Cubby's size," said Papa. "I may have lost it myself. Ma used to say I was a terrible one to strut around." Papa laughed and rubbed Cubby's head. "I must have wanted to show off my pretty curls."

"Just like Cubby," Honey murmured sleepily.

Cubby gave her a halfhearted kick on the shin. Honey tried to return the kick but Papa caught their feet in his big hand.

"Are you going to hunt for Spanish gold, young fellow?" he asked.

"Nope," said Cubby. "I'm going to hunt Grand-pappy Bundie's ghost."

"What would you do if you found it?" Papa said teasingly.

"I'd walk right up to it and I'd say—"

"Put me to bed," interrupted Honey. "I need sleep."

Papa laughed and carried the twins into the house. Mamma went along to see that they washed their feet before they went to bed. Len and Glory stayed on the porch watching the shadows.

"Len," said Glory wistfully. "There's nothing to be afraid of in the cave."

"I reckon there isn't," he answered. "Maybe I've been foolish and stubborn."

"Then you really mean we'll go?"

Glory could hardly believe she was listening to Len.

"Yes," he said slowly. "Seeing that you're so set on it, we'll go."

"When? Tomorrow?"

"We'll go to Granny's first and get the rugs. Then we'll come back by the cave."

"Cross your heart?"

Len Makes a Promise

"Cross my heart and hope to die," Len promised.

Glory was so excited when she went to bed that she didn't notice Miss Nancy Rose's basket was still empty.

6

Granny Baker

GLORY'S BUCKET banged against her knees with every step she took as she followed Len down Wolf Hill. It hurt like fury but she didn't take time to rub the pain away. Len already acted sorry that he had promised to take her to the cave. He might change his mind if she complained—even if he had crossed his heart and hoped to die.

"Len," she called, hoping to slow down his long legs. "Where do you suppose Miss Nancy Rose was last night? She wasn't in her basket at all."

"Not far away," Len called back. "She was Johnny-on-the-spot when I milked this morning."

"She disappeared again right after breakfast," said Glory. "How do you suppose she got to the haunted house in the first place?"

"Witches," Len answered. "Maybe the same old witch that lives in Witch Cave."

"Shucks," Glory said, laughing in spite of an extra hard bump from the bucket. "If you really believed a witch lived in the cave, you'd never be going there this afternoon. Besides, it's a ghost, not a witch."

"Ghost or witch or conjure woman, it's all one and the same," Len answered.

"You know you don't really believe that stuff," Glory said.

Len shrugged his shoulders and changed the conversation.

"How many rugs do you suppose Granny has to sell this time?"

"More than last time, I hope," said Glory. "She'll never get that new pair of shoes that she's needed for so long if she doesn't."

Granny was famous for her handwoven rugs. Even beyond the mountains folks knew about them.

51

Miss Annie who owned the gift shop at Lone Pine sold them to tourists.

Miss Annie was always scolding Granny for traipsing over the countryside nursing sick folks who couldn't pay cash for her work. Granny only laughed and at the next call for help she'd be off with her basket of medicines.

Glory thought Miss Annie was right but, gracious, what would folks do if there were no Granny to help in time of sickness? It was true that she needed money and her friends could give her little. A smoked ham, a bushel of potatoes, corn for her cow—these things were her pay. But there were things that took money. Shoes for instance and coal oil for her lamps.

At Deer Creek, Glory and Len stopped to cool their feet in the water before they started up Deer Knob. A red bird darted from a tree and perched on a bush in front of them.

"Quick, Glory, make a wish," cried Len. "There's a red bird."

Glory shut her eyes. A red bird wish was the luckiest of them all. This wish must be good.

"What did you wish for? Spanish gold?" Len asked when she opened her eyes.

Glory shook her head. She had wished they'd see Grandpappy Bundie's ghost but she didn't dare tell Len. Not that she thought it was real but she wanted to see the thing that had kept Grandpappy talking for all these years.

"It won't come true if I tell," she said. "Come on. There's Granny waiting for us."

Granny's cabin was a pretty sight with dogwood and wild plum trees crowded close around. Glory thought it was the prettiest place for miles, no matter which way a person went. Especially in the spring when the trees were in blossom, making the hillside a regular flower garden.

The cabin was old—as old as Granny Baker's father—and the logs were weathered to silver smoothness. The chimney was covered with a trumpet vine so big it hid the roof and swung in the wind on the other side of the house.

Granny waited with the door open while they were still a long way off. She was a spry little woman, thin and quick as a small brown bird. Her white hair was twisted in a tight knot at the back of her head. Her gray starched dress was covered with a more stiffly starched apron.

"I knew within reason I'd have company today,"

she called. "The rooster crowed all morning at the back door. I made up a pan of gingerbread just to be ready when the company came."

She flapped her apron to hold back the flies that clung to the screen door.

"There's bound to be a change in the weather," she said. "The flies want to come in."

"It could be they like gingerbread," Len said, sniffing the hot spicy odor that filled the room.

Glory and Len set the berries on the table and Granny motioned them to chairs while she cut the gingerbread into large squares.

"I'm beholden to you for the berries," she said as she passed the gingerbread. "It's hot stooping over berry bushes in this sun."

"We were glad to pick them for you," replied Len. "Granny, you make the best gingerbread I ever ate."

"Go along, boy," Granny said but smiling proudly all the while. "Have another piece."

"Thank you, ma'am." Len helped himself to another piece.

"What's new in the neighborhood?" Granny asked.

"Glory's cat," he answered with his mouth full.

"A stray. Papa and Mamma had a fit when she brought it home."

"And Len," Glory added, grinning at Granny. She went on to tell of finding the cat at the haunted house. "She was hungry and lonesome. She's not like any cat you ever saw."

"Seems like I heard of a tourist losing a cat sometime back," Granny said thoughtfully. "She made a great to-do about it. She even offered an outlandish reward. Folks thought she was downright addlepated to make such a fuss over a cat."

Glory listened uneasily. She hadn't thought that someone might have lost the cat. That someone might love her enough to offer money for her return. Glory had supposed that Miss Nancy Rose had purposely been left behind by someone who was afraid to move a cat.

"Where did she lose it?" she asked anxiously. "Near the haunted house?"

"Law, child, I didn't bother my mind to remember," Granny replied. "As well as I can recollect it was beyond Rocky Ridge."

"Oh, that's miles away." Glory's uneasiness vanished. "Miss Nancy Rose can't be her cat."

"Where are your rugs, Granny?" asked Len. Now

that he had made up his mind to go to Witch Cave
he didn't want to waste time talking about Glory's
cat. "I hope you've made enough to satisfy Miss
Annie."

"I don't think that could be possible," said
Granny. "Jake Miller's broken leg set me back some.
I've only made four."

"That won't bring you much cash," said Len. He
looked at Granny anxiously. "Come winter, you'll
need things. Maybe you should spend more time on
your weaving. Money is hard to come by."

"That's true, Len," answered Granny. "I'd be digging a mighty hard row of stumps if I didn't get cash
money for my weaving. But my real work is nursing
the sick. I've got no hankering to change."

"But your friends can't pay you money," said Len
earnestly. "We're all as poor as Job's turkey."

"You're a great one to talk," said Granny. "Any
time you've a mind to you can stand on the highway
and get fifty cents a bucket for those berries. But
what do you do? You bring them to me so I won't go
hungry this winter."

Len's face flushed.

"I couldn't sell the berries when you need them,"

he said. "I wouldn't feel right about taking the money."

"That's what I mean," said Granny seriously. "Folks here are bound together in friendship. It's more important than money in our pockets. No more would I get pleasure from my rug money if I set it above the needs of my friends."

Len and Glory turned Granny's words over in their minds. It was true. Here in the hills, the trouble of one was the trouble of all. Sudden need brought neighbors close together.

Men plowed fields that were not their own. They planted the seeds and harvested the crops so a sick man's family would not feel the pinch of want. Women carried food to those in trouble. There wasn't a family in the hills that hadn't received help. Nor one that had not gone out of the way to bring comfort to their neighbors.

Len studied Granny's face, wrinkled as a dried apple. She was little. So little he could look over her head but she was strong enough to carry the burdens of her people. Granny wasn't poor. She was rich in the riches she held dear.

"I see what you mean," he said, lifting the bundle

of rugs to his shoulder. "I'm proud to be your friend."

"Do you have to go?" asked Granny as she followed them to the door.

"We're going back by Witch Cave," said Glory. "We're going to explore it."

"Don't let the haunts carry you off," said Granny and she laughed at their startled faces.

"Do you believe those stories?" asked Len.

"I can't say I do," she said. Her eyes were serious. "Still, there are things in this world that are past our understanding."

Glory and Len turned away. Things past our understanding. Glory wished Granny hadn't said that.

"What do you suppose she meant by that?" asked Len.

"I don't know," said Glory. "But I'm not going to worry about it."

A cloud passed over the sun. The trail grew shadowy. A sudden gust of wind set a small dust devil whirling in the path ahead of them. Both Glory and Len stepped aside. Neither of them would do anything so foolish as to run through a dust devil. Len felt in his pocket for his rabbit foot.

7

Grandpappy's Ghost

LEN AND GLORY stopped at the edge of Witch Hollow. Here the valley widened between Wolf Hill and Deer Knob, forming a small grassy meadow where the neighborhood cows liked to graze. Granny's Cindy was there quietly chewing her cud under a sweet gum tree. Len looked around for their own Mayflower but she wasn't in sight. He was glad. He always dreaded to come here for her at milking time.

Ordinarily Glory liked to come here but today it

didn't seem the same. Perhaps it was because of the wind and the darkening clouds or perhaps it was only her imagination but Witch Hollow seemed strange and unfamiliar.

Long ago some settler had built his cabin in the hollow. All that was left of it now was the stone chimney and the wide stone hearth. Even Grandpappy Bundie who was the oldest person for miles around didn't know who had built the cabin nor what had happened to it. Struck by lightning, he said. Or maybe Deer Creek had risen and washed it away. Of the people who had once lived there— not a fragment of their story lingered in the minds of the old folks. So the chimney and the grassy hollow had become a part of the Witch Cave legend, a place to be shunned after the sun went down.

The trail divided at the creek and became two trails. One led along the right bank and joined an old road which twisted around the south side of the hill. This road was seldom used except by two or three families who lived on the far side of Deer Knob and folks who stopped at Granny's cabin.

The other path led across the creek on teetery stepping stones and skirted the foot of Wolf Hill. At this point the hill was a wall of rocks and the trail became a footpath which ran along a narrow ledge for almost a hundred feet. Then it turned abruptly and climbed a natural stairway of rocks. To the right of the stairway, facing Deer Creek, lay the black opening of Witch Cave.

Today Glory didn't stay behind as she usually did to wonder about the chimney and the cabin that had once stood there. Len's foot was hardly off one slippery stone before hers was in its place. The rising wind tugged at her faded dress.

"The wind has changed," she said. "Do you think it will rain?"

Len studied the scudding clouds.

"We don't usually get a rain when the wind is in this direction. I doubt it will rain right off."

Although the sun had dropped behind Deer Knob and long shadows covered the trail, the stones in front of the cave were still warm to the children's feet. The entrance was bigger and blacker than Glory had remembered. She thought of her red bird wish and glanced upward. No misty white thing sailed out over her head. She hadn't expected it but it was just as well.

Len laid Granny's bundle of rugs on the stones at the bottom of the stairway. Pulling a handful of candle ends and some matches from his pocket he handed them to Glory.

"You take these," he said. "I have my flashlight."

Len pressed the button. In the dim circle of light they could see rough stones arching high above their heads. Rocks jutted out from the walls which seemed to widen into a large room at the rear of the cave. Len moved the flash trying to pierce the darkness but the small bit of light was lost in the immense blackness.

"Light the candles," he said. "We should have brought the lantern but I had no idea the place would be so big."

Glory struck a match and held it to the candle wick. The match flame flickered and went out. A second match did the same. Glory turned her back to the cave trying to protect the wavering flame from the wind.

The wind suddenly shifted and increased in force. Len cupped his hands around the candle while Glory struck another match. Then a low moaning sound came from the cave. At first faint and far away, it grew steadily louder until the moan became a wail and the wail became a wild shriek.

The candles fell from Glory's hands as she stared

63

at Len, too frightened to move. She shivered as his cold fingers closed around her wrist.

Then as it had come, it died away. A quavering moan, then—silence. The woods were still. Even the leaves ceased rustling.

For an instant they stood, their hearts pounding in their ears. All at once they were seized by unreasoning panic. They raced up the stairway and fled along the ridge trail, never stopping until they could see their own chimney top rising above the trees.

"Wait," Glory panted. "I've got to rest. I've got a stitch in my side."

She flopped down on a log beside the path and closed her eyes. Len, exhausted and out of breath, threw himself on the ground.

"Wh-what was it?" asked Glory. "Grandpappy's ghost?"

Len's face was still pale but he managed a sickly grin.

"I didn't wait to see," he laughed. "But for a girl who isn't afraid of ghosts, you made a speedy getaway. I bet you broke some sort of record."

Glory giggled and wiped her hot face on her dress.

"I'm not really afraid," she explained. "I was only running for my health."

"Yeah," said Len. "Your health wasn't so good around that ca—"

There was a rustling in the bushes. Something warm and wet slapped Len across the cheek.

"Ow-eee—ee."

Len's squawk echoed across the hills. He covered his face with one arm and struck out wildly with the other. His fist cracked against something solid. A terrifying bellow and another swipe across the ear pushed him backwards. He tried to roll but he only succeeded in wedging himself firmly between a blackberry bush and a big boulder.

Again came that horrible bawl, this time close in his ear. Frightened as he was, Len thought there was something familiar about that noise. He opened one eye, just the merest slit.

A brown hairy head hung over him. Two friendly eyes peered into his. He ducked his head as May-flower's long tongue once more swung in his direction.

"Get out of here, you sorry old beast," he cried, giving the cow a kick which hurt his own toe. "I hope you bite your tongue clean off before you scare the living daylights out of me again. Glory! Help me up."

But Glory couldn't help anyone up. She was stretched out on the log, tears of laughter rolling down her cheeks.

"Oh. Oh. I never saw anything so funny."

"Oh—you never did," growled Len, trying to untangle a blackberry branch from the back of his shirt. "Just sit and enjoy yourself then. I'm going home."

He gave Mayflower a sharp slap across the back and started her down the trail. The cow walked slowly, switching her tail and snatching at the leaves on the low bushes. Not once did Len look back as he followed but he knew Glory was behind him. He could hear her laughing.

Neither of them remembered Granny's bundle of rugs on the rocks by Witch Cave.

8

A Broken Promise

LEN TOOK the cow to the barn and went about the milking. Miss Nancy Rose who was washing her paws on the step saw Glory and scampered across the yard to meet her. Glory picked her up and held her close for a minute before she went in to help Mamma with the supper.

The twins had already set the table and were stretched out on the floor looking at the new mail order catalogue. Glory was glad that Mamma seemingly had forgotten about their trip to the cave. She only looked up from the cornbread she was stirring and smiled. Glory washed her hands and began to help about the stove where the food was cooking in big pots. At times Mamma's forgetfulness was a real help.

Later when they were all seated about the table with the lamplight shining on Mamma's tired face, with Papa's and Cubby's heads gleaming like new pennies, their fears seemed foolish. The cry at the cave was unreal.

"Did you find the Spanish gold?" asked Papa, taking Cubby's spoon away from Honey's pie.

Glory choked on a swallow of buttermilk. Mamma might forget but depend on Papa.

"Ah—uh—no," said Len with a sidelong glance at Glory. "We sort of—well, you might say we left too soon."

Papa looked at their red faces and laughed.

"Did Grandpappy Bundie's ghost scare you?" he exclaimed. "You didn't see it!"

"No, we didn't see it," confessed Glory. "We heard it, but you know we're pretty fast runners."

The twins' spoons stopped midway to their open mouths. Cubby's eyes glistened expectantly.

"What'd you see, Glory?" he shouted. "Take me. I want to see too."

"Hush, Cubby." Mamma laid her hand on his shoulder. "Let them talk."

"Glory's not afraid of ghosts," began Len.

"Or cows," Glory added.

At that moment the door opened and Granny Baker came into the kitchen. Papa drew up another chair and Mamma got a clean plate.

"You're just in time to have a bite with us," she said happily as she dished up warm food.

"I can't stay," said Granny, "but that blackberry pie looks mighty tempting. I just stopped to ask Len if he'd look after Cindy for a few days. Sam Black came after me. His wife's sick and the baby is ailing. He needs help pretty bad. I don't know how long I'll be gone but everything will be all right down at my place except the cow. Don't bother with the chickens. I turned them out to fend for themselves."

"I'll be proud to look after Cindy for you," said Len. "I'll bring her up here and put her with Mayflower."

Granny turned to go and Mamma took an extra

70

pie from the cupboard. She wrapped it in a clean towel and handed it to Granny.

"Take it with you," she said. "It isn't much but it's filling."

They all followed Granny to the yard where Sam Black waited in his pickup truck. Mamma asked about the sick ones and kindly offered to help if she was needed. Sam thanked her and stepped on the starter. Granny leaned out and called above the rattle of the engine.

"Len, don't bother to take those rugs down to Miss Annie's while it's so warm. Wait 'til your pa goes. There's no hurry."

Sam drove away before Len could answer. The rugs. They had forgotten them!

"Len," Glory whispered. "We left them—"

"I know where we left them," he answered sharply.

Len went back to the steps and sat with his head in his hands. Glory huddled beside him. She looked out at the woods, now completely dark. Lightning flashed over Deer Knob. The storm which had threatened all the afternoon was almost upon them. Granny's rugs down on the rocks would be ruined

They couldn't leave them there. Not when Granny needed money so badly.

Yet Glory turned cold at the thought of going down the ridge trail again—down to the cave with that horrible noise.

"Do we have to go tonight?"

Glory knew the answer without Len's impatient reply.

"You know we have to get them tonight. We promised, didn't we?"

They had promised but all the same a promise didn't make the woods less dark or Witch Cave less frightening.

"You don't have to go," Len said gruffly. "I forgot them."

"I forgot them too." Glory knew why Len was so sharp and gruff. He was afraid too, just as frightened as she was. "I'll go with you."

The light from Sam's truck disappeared over the hill and Mamma and the twins went into the house. Papa stopped beside Glory and Len, crouched on the steps.

"What's the matter with you young ones?" he asked curiously. "Are you sick?"

A Broken Promise

"We left Granny's rugs down by the cave," said Len. "We're just going after them."

Len knew how Papa felt about a broken promise. He felt the same way himself. He had given his word and Granny depended on him. He got up slowly and reached in his pocket for his flashlight. It was gone. He and Glory started for the gate.

"Wait a minute." Papa looked at the sky. The clouds were rolling low over the mountain tops. "Get the lantern, Len," he said. "Glory, go help your mother with the dishes. I'll go with him."

Papa and Len started back over the trail. In the bobbing light Len could see Papa's feet and part of his blue overalled legs. That was enough. He would follow those feet anywhere they led him.

Glory was on the porch when they came back. Len thought she was waiting for them.

"We found them," he called. "You don't need to worry any more."

But Glory wasn't worrying about the rugs now. She knew Papa would find them.

"Len, Miss Nancy Rose is gone again. She ate her supper and disappeared. She'll be out in the storm."

"That silly cat of yours is way down by the cave," he said. "I tried to catch her but she wouldn't let

me come near her. She dodged around rocks and bushes and then disappeared right before my eyes. Craziest thing I ever saw. There she was and then—there she wasn't."

He quickly pulled one of her braids.

"She's a ghost cat, I tell you," he whispered with his eyes on Papa's back. "She disappears after the sun sets. Just like—you know who."

9

Trouble for Granny

THE LONG-LOOKED-FOR rain came in the night.
Lightning made the sky bright as day and thunder
rolled along the ridges and echoed in the hollows.
Glory pulled the sheet up over her head and tried
to shut out the blinding flashes.

She thought of Miss Nancy Rose out in the woods,
alone and wet. Once she slipped out of bed and
opened the door but she couldn't see anything in
the storm.

The thunder woke Honey and Cubby. They scur-

ried across the room and jumped in bed with Glory.

"Don't be afraid," she said. "Listen. It's the Old Man in the Sky driving his apple cart across the bridge."

"There. He spilled 'em," said Cubby as the thunder rattled across the sky.

Honey yawned loudly.

"I wish I could eat a thunder apple. Glory, what do thunder apples taste like? I bet they're good. Tomorrow I'm going to hunt me—a—thunder—apple." Honey was asleep.

Cubby was restless. First he was too cold. Then he was too hot. He drew up his knees and punched Glory in the back. He wanted a piece of left-over pie. He wanted a drink of water.

"You don't need that stuff," Glory said impatiently. "Now be still."

Cubby was still for almost thirty seconds.

"How old is the Old Man in the Sky?" he asked.

"I don't know."

Glory kicked back the sheet but by now Cubby was cold and wanted it pulled up again.

"Glory, is the Old Man in the Sky as old as Grandpappy Bundie?"

"Older."

"That would make him as old as Santy Claus, wouldn't it?"

"Probably. Go to sleep."

Cubby was still for a whole minute and Glory thought he was asleep. Then he punched her in the back again.

"Do you think the Old Man in the Sky can spit tobacco juice through a knothole like Jake Wheeler?"

"He doesn't have any tobacco juice." Glory was heartily sick of the Old Man in the Sky. "Be still, can't you?"

"He could spit apple juice," Cubby said after considering the matter for some time. "Apple juice spits real good."

Glory gritted her teeth to keep from answering. Cubby waited, punched her again, drew a long sigh and went to sleep.

By this time Glory was wide awake. She kept seeing a little white cat hiding under bushes, crouching behind stones, seeking a shelter from the wind and rain. She blamed Len for leaving her down by the cave. If only she had gone with them Miss Nancy Rose would now be safe in the barn.

Glory was hot and uncomfortable with the twins

crowding close. Once she thought she would go over into their bed but when she moved they clung to her. She lay down again, knowing they were afraid of the storm even in their sleep.

The continuous flashes of lightning filled the sky with a steady glow. The thunder echoed and re-echoed through the hills. Finally Glory went to sleep but a little lost cat wandered in and out of her dreams.

The rain was still falling the next morning. Deer Knob was capped with white clouds and the hollows were filled with gray mist that hid the trees.

Glory was delighted to see Miss Nancy Rose waiting at the door. She warmed a pan of milk and the bedraggled cat lapped it hungrily. After she had eaten Glory rubbed her with a towel and brushed her tangled hair. She seemed none the worse for her night in the woods.

No one hurried at breakfast. It was like a holiday, Glory thought, a holiday to celebrate the coming of the rain. Mamma opened a jar of strawberry jam to eat with their hot biscuits.

At last Papa pushed back his chair and left to do the barn work. Len put on his oldest clothes and started down the trail to get Granny's cow.

The rain had brought relief from the heat so Mamma decided this would be a good day to make jam. She put more wood in the stove and set a kettle of blackberries to cook. Glory went to the smoke-house and dug through a box for jelly glasses.

"Can't Miss Nancy Rose come in?" begged Cubby. "The poor little wet kitty."

"No, she can't come in," answered Mamma, dipping up a cup of sugar and pouring it into the kettle.

"She's not a stray any more," argued Honey. "She's Glory's beautiful Miss Nancy Rose. You wouldn't shut Glory out in the rain if she was lost and I found her."

Mamma didn't answer. She went on dipping up cups of sugar and laying aside a berry for each cup. Sometimes with all the racket in the house Mamma lost count. The berries helped her keep track.

Cubby watched the boiling sugar turn pink and bubble up to the top of the kettle. Mamma skimmed off the foam and put it in a dish. Cubby wanted to eat it but Mamma was afraid the foam was filled with impurities from the berries and might make him sick.

Cubby turned away and flattened his nose against

the window pane. He cupped his hands around his face and peered out through the rain.

"Something's the matter with Len," he said. "He's running fast."

Cubby dashed to the porch, slamming the door behind him.

"Is Grandpappy's ghost chasing you?" he shouted. "Bring it in the house."

Len pushed Cubby aside.

"Mamma," he cried. "Granny's house was struck by lightning last night. It burned clean to the ground."

Mamma dropped the big wooden spoon which hit the edge of the kettle and clattered to the floor. She sat down in a chair, her face pale and her shoulders drooping with the thought of this trouble that had come upon Granny.

For once the twins were still. They squeezed into a chair and sat with their fingers in their mouths—feeling the trouble but not understanding it.

The berries boiled over on the stove, filling the room with smoke. Glory moved the kettle to a cooler place. Lifting the lid she scraped the blackened sugar into the fire. Mamma didn't notice.

"Len, go call your father," she said.

Len caught Papa as he was driving out of the yard on his way to the market at Lone Pine with a load of watermelons. He came in and listened while Len told his story again. There really wasn't much to tell. The cabin was gone with everything in it. The chimney, all that was left, was cracked from top to bottom. The barn was still standing. Cindy was bawling to be milked. The chickens were pecking around the yard, already scratching in the wet ashes.

"The loom too?" asked Glory. "Is it gone?"

"Everything," said Len. "There's only a heap of ashes left."

"What will Granny do?" she asked.

It was only yesterday that Granny said she would be digging a hard row of stumps if she didn't have her rug money. And now, with no house, with everything she owned lost in the blaze, Granny would really be hard put to make ends meet.

"Well," said Mamma, jumping up from her chair. "It's not for Granny to do anything right now. It's for us, her friends, to get busy. Cubby, get the mop and wipe up the water on the floor. I can't abide a tracked-up floor. I can't think when I've got my mind on a spot of mud. Honey, climb up on the box

83

and wash the jars. Glory, put the berries back on the stove and watch this time. Don't let them burn. Papa, instead of taking those melons to market, you go to Sam Black's and tell Granny what has happened. She might better have the bad news from us. Stop at everybody's house along the way and tell them Granny's in trouble. Len—"

But Len was already down the trail. He brought Cindy back and gave her an extra dip of bran to make her feel at home. Then he turned her loose with Mayflower.

It was late in the afternoon when Papa came back. Granny had taken the news with her usual calmness. Everywhere Papa had gone folks were saddened by the news. The women had turned away from him to search among their few belongings for things that could be spared for Granny. Everyone was of one mind. The cabin should be rebuilt at once.

10

A Gift for Granny

FOR SEVERAL DAYS after the fire Len and Glory were in a dither of excitement and worry. They were excited because Granny's new cabin had gone up almost like magic, with the men in the neighborhood working each day until dark drove them home. But their spirits were low when they thought of the housewarming party to be given when the cabin was finished. Folks would come from near and far and all would have a fine gift for Granny.

Women were already scurrying about from house

to house, collecting furniture where it could be spared. Mamma had an old table which she had painted green. There was only one little spot to mar its shining beauty. That was the mark of Cubby's tongue. He had wondered if wet paint tasted as good as it looked.

But Mamma's table hadn't solved the gift problem for Glory and Len. Glory's mind was a confused blank when she tried to think of something. Len's was no better. They argued and fretted, never agreeing on anything, until Mamma was completely worn out with their bickering and noise.

Then one day they found the answer in a most unexpected place. Right in the middle of the highway Len found a pink handbill that advertised a farm sale over at Oak Summit. Among other things listed for sale was an old loom. That was it. The perfect gift to take the place of the loom Granny had lost.

Of course that meant money and asking Papa for it was out of reason. There was never enough money at their house to spread over coats and shoes and overalls as it was, let alone a big thing like a loom for Granny.

For one whole day Glory's mind went round and

round like a squirrel in a cage. Then suddenly she remembered that Granny had said people would pay fifty cents a gallon for blackberries. Len didn't believe they would but the first gallon sold so quickly that they were hardly out of the patch before they were back. At the end of the day they had earned a dollar and fifty cents.

Each night they took down the old cracked sugar bowl and poured their money on the table. The pile of dimes and quarters and half dollars grew bigger and bigger. Last night they had counted nine whole dollars. That was a lot of money. Plenty to buy an old loom.

But Papa was doubtful. It all depended on how many folks were interested in the loom. If no one but Len and Glory wanted it nine dollars would be plenty. All they could do was wait and see.

It was a good thing the sale was tomorrow. Glory knew she would burst if she had to wait much longer. She wished she were like Cubby and Honey. They never bothered about tomorrow nor remembered yesterday. There they were, squeezed in the old tire swing, giggling over some private joke. And Len, out in the garden calmly chopping weeds. But here she was, twisting and turning and fairly wearing out her dress tail on the back steps while she watched the twins.

If Mamma were only home she could be out doing something. Picking more berries and earning another fifty cents. But Mamma was over at Mrs. Miller's piecing comforts for Granny's bed and Glory wasn't supposed to let Honey and Cubby out of her sight.

She thought of all that money in the sugar bowl. Nine dollars. More than she and Len had had in their whole lives before. Surely it would be enough for an old secondhand loom—enough and some to spare, if no one else wanted it.

But suppose someone did. Someone who could bid nine dollars and fifty cents. The more she thought of that fifty cents the more certain she was that they should have one more gallon of blackberries. But what to do with the twins. They'd be a nuisance in the berry patch. She pumped a cup of water and took it out to Len.

"Len," she said. "I'm afraid nine dollars won't be enough. What do you say we take the twins up on Wolf Hill while we pick more berries? Do you suppose they'll be good?"

Len leaned on his hoe and studied the twins. He

was tired of chopping weeds, and picking berries for the loom was the only excuse Papa would take if he should stop work.

"If they aren't good we can bring them home," Glory added.

"Hey, kids," Len called. "Come here."

"What for?" said Cubby, not moving from the swing.

"Will you be good if we take you with us to pick berries?"

Cubby thought the question over carefully. He looked at Honey. They grinned mischievously.

"We'll be good for cookies," he bargained.

"We'll be good for five," said Honey. "We won't be good if we can't have five."

"I wish I was that smart," sighed Len, wiping his hot face on his sleeve.

"All right," said Glory. "But mind. Only five."

The twins scrambled out of the swing. At the door Cubby turned.

"How many is five?" he called.

"You know," replied Glory. "One for each finger."

She got the buckets and waited at the gate with Len but the twins didn't appear.

"They've had plenty of time to get five cookies," said Glory.

"Let 'em alone," answered Len. "They've got to learn to count."

Nevertheless Glory started back to the house. Cubby opened the door with his foot. Glory eyed them sternly. Their hands were full. Their pockets were stuffed and their cheeks bulged like squirrels' loaded with walnuts.

"I told you five," scolded Glory. "You took more."

Cubby shook his head, gulped and swallowed.

"I counted just the way you said. One for each finger."

"How many hands did you each hold up?" demanded Glory.

"All both of them," mumbled Honey with a crumby grin. "I like the way Cubby counts. This is the most we ever got for five."

"You and your counting lesson," said Glory, turning to Len who was laughing in a most annoying way.

"It's your fault," he said, opening the gate that led to the ridge trail. "You should have said just one hand."

"From the looks of them I think they counted their toes too," she said.

There weren't as many berries on the hill as Glory had hoped for. She and Len wandered in and out among the bushes, the twins trailing behind, but the buckets filled slowly.

That extra fifty cents became more important and Glory picked with growing haste. It took a lot of berries to buy a loom but it would be worth all the scratched legs and chigger bites when it was placed in Granny's cabin by the window—just where the old one had stood. But the place wouldn't look the same without Granny's familiar things.

There would be no white dishes scattered over with little brown leaves. The bed wouldn't be the same without the blue coverlet that Granny's mother had woven so long ago. Glory had tried to tell Granny how she felt but the old woman had only patted her shoulder.

"Law, child," she had said. "They were only things. They weren't matters of the spirit. I don't need a coverlet to remember my mother. As for the dishes, I've always had a hankering for some of those flowery ones from the Five-and-Ten. They'd look mighty pretty lined up on my new shelves. Kind of like a flower garden right inside my house."

Glory knew there was little chance of Granny getting the flowery dishes. She'd probably have a plate from one family and a cup from another, no two alike, yet Granny would be happy with them.

"I'm tired," said Honey, interrupting Glory's thoughts. "I want to go home."

"Just a little while more, Honey," said Glory. "Don't you want to help?"

"No, she doesn't," answered Cubby decidedly. "She's tired."

"Would you like to go back to the trail?" asked Len. "You could wait for us there."

"We'll wait," said Honey, and Cubby nodded.

"Promise?" asked Glory. "Cross your heart?"

"Promise," said Honey and Cubby, crossing their stomachs.

]]

Cubby Hunts a Ghost

FOR A TIME Cubby and Honey sat on the log where Len put them. They could see him moving in and out among the bushes. Glory was farther away but they could see her too when she climbed up on a rock and waved to them. The shade was cool and pleasant. Honey missed her afternoon nap. She yawned and stretched out on the log.

Cubby's eyes were heavy too but he wouldn't think of taking a nap unless Mamma made him. He slipped off the log, gathered a handful of stones and began to pile them in little heaps along the path.

Suddenly, right by his big toe, he saw a long line of ants. They were running across the trail, over the stones and into the tall grass.

"I wonder where they're going so fast," he said. "Their mamma must be calling them."

He crawled along beside the ants, his nose close to the ground. The weeds scratched his bare feet and the sharp stones hurt his knees but he followed the ants until they disappeared down a hole under a bush.

Cubby watched them curiously. He had never seen such busy ants before. Some were running into the hole. Some were running out. He brushed aside the leaves to get a better view. There, half hidden by a stone, he saw the gleam of shining metal. A wide grin spread over his face. His fingers closed around Len's flashlight.

"Look, Honey," he said, shaking her awake. "Look what I found."

"That's Len's," she said. She yawned and rubbed her sleepy eyes. "He's hunted for that every day. We've got to take it to him."

"He told us to stay here," Cubby reminded her as

he glanced quickly toward the bushes where Len was working.

He snapped the button several times. He held the light close to his eye to see if it worked.

"Len will be mad," cautioned Honey. "He doesn't let us play with his flashlight."

"I know it." But Cubby didn't think Len would be too mad. "He'll be so glad I found it he might say we could play with it."

"I don't think he will," said Honey doubtfully.

Cubby stood up and looked toward the bushes. Len saw him and waved.

"O.K., Cubby?" he called.

"O.K.," Cubby answered carelessly.

He watched Len return to his work. He looked around for Glory but he couldn't see her. With a stubborn glance at Honey, he started down the trail. At the top of the hill where the stone stairway led to Witch Cave he sat down. Honey sat down beside him and looked longingly at the flashlight.

"It's my turn now," she said, snatching it from his hand.

"Wait a minute, can't you?"

Cubby jerked it away from her and turned his back.

"I'm going to tell Len," she threatened. "I'll tell him right now if you don't give it to me."

"Please wait 'til we see it in the dark," pleaded Cubby. "We won't have another chance."

"There's some dark."

Honey pointed to the black opening of Witch Cave. Cubby studied it a long time.

"I'll bet that's where Grandpappy Bundie's ghost lives," he said. "Let's scare it out."

The air was cold at the cave entrance. Honey pulled her thin shirt together where a couple of buttons were missing. Cubby snapped on the light. The spot made a faint circle on the stone wall.

"What's a ghost, Cubby?" asked Honey.

"I don't know," he answered. "Something funny because Papa laughed when Glory and Len were afraid. But I'm not afraid of the darkest dark there is."

Cubby started forward, the round circle of light bobbing uncertainly in front of him. Honey, holding tightly to the straps of his overalls, was close beside him.

It was only a moment before they reached the back of the cave. Cubby was disappointed. He was

sure that somewhere in the darkness was the ghost that had chased Glory and Len home.

He moved the light about the high walls. To the right he saw an opening like a long hallway. Here the floor slanted slightly and in the dim glow of the spot Cubby thought there might be another room beyond. The light faded into nothingness in the blackness. He could still see the bright sunlight at the entrance when he turned around but the darkness ahead was like none he had ever known.

"I see something," said Honey, pointing down the passage to the right.

The spot of light showed a heap of dried leaves and on the leaves lay something white. The twins left the main room of the cave and followed the narrow passage.

"We've found the ghost, Cubby. Look."

Honey carefully picked up the small object and turned to Cubby. Her elbow struck the flashlight and sent it bounding across the floor. The light went out. In the darkness the twins listened as the flashlight rolled farther and farther away over the uneven stones.

12

Miss Nancy Rose
Leads the Way

LEN WORKED ALONG, whistling to himself. He was a fast picker and when he came to a heavily loaded bush he began stripping the berries with both hands. He was so interested he forgot all about the twins until he heard Glory call.

"Len. Come quick. They're gone."

He set his bucket down and ran crashing through the underbrush. Glory was running about looking under bushes and behind rocks. On the log where

Honey had rested they found a half-eaten cookie. Cubby's piles of stones were just as he had left them.

"Do you suppose they got tired and went home?" asked Glory anxiously.

"They'd have told us," said Len. "I think they're right around here. They haven't had time to go far."

"Here's another cookie. They went this way," called Glory, running along the trail toward the cave.

On the stone stairway a blue jay pecked at a bit of food. It was another cookie.

"Thank goodness Cubby couldn't count," said Len. "We'll find them if their cookies hold out."

But the cookie trail stopped on the ledge by the cave. They searched the green depths of the water, their throats tight with fear. Only a few fish lay motionless at the bottom of the pool. Len and Glory turned away in relief. At least they weren't down there.

"Cubb-eeeee." Len sent the call echoing across the hills. "Honey."

From the cave behind them came a roar so horrible that Len's scalp prickled and cold chills chased up and down his spine. Glory sank to the rocks, her knees too weak to hold her up. Something soft and warm landed in her lap. She screamed, but it was only Miss Nancy Rose.

"Wh-what's that?" gasped Len.

"I don't know," replied Glory and she covered her ears as the roar sounded again.

Miss Nancy Rose leaped from her lap and ran toward the cave. When Glory made no move to follow, the cat came back and clawed at her dress.

"What's the matter with you?" said Glory as the cat dodged away from her hands and sat down in the entrance of the cave. "She wants something. She acts as if she wants us to go with her."

"Maybe she does," exclaimed Len. He ran to the cave. "Cubby! Honey!" he called.

The answer was another roar.

"Are you all right?" Roar. "Is Honey with you?" Roar.

"What makes them sound like that?" asked Glory with a bewildered look.

"It's the echo—I think," replied Len. He called again to Cubby. "Stay where you are. Don't move around. I'm coming after you."

Len's face was pale but his mouth was grimly determined as he turned to Glory.

"You're crazy," cried Glory. "You can't go in there without a light. Wait. I'll go home for the lantern."

"I can't wait. Those kids are in there alone." Len hoped he sounded braver than he felt. The cave was frightfully black. "Go to Granny's cabin and bring Papa. There'll be lanterns there. Some of the men were going to work late tonight."

He hesitated, trying to bring himself to plunge into the yawning darkness.

"Wait. I've got an idea." Glory tore the thin belt from her dress. She knelt down and tied one end around Miss Nancy Rose's neck. "Now see if she will lead you in," she said, handing the other end to Len. "She can see in the dark."

The cat meowed excitedly and trotted into the cave.

"I wish I had cat eyes," said Len. "I don't want to pitch over anything in there. G'by. I'll see you later."

Following the gentle pull on the belt he stepped into the cave. The darkest night in the woods was nothing to the blackness that closed around Len. He shuffled along, feeling his way, afraid to lift his feet for fear of those unexpected cracks into which a person could fall and disappear forever. Ledges—

underground streams—bottomless pits. Len tried to control his mounting fear but his teeth began to chatter.

All the stories he had heard about Witch Cave crowded into his mind. The Spaniards with their plundered gold. Grandpa's train robbers. Grandpappy Bundie's ghost. They leered at him in the darkness as he inched along behind a cat he could not see.

Once he called but his voice came back, bouncing from wall to wall. Echo piled upon echo until his words became a jumble of mocking sounds. He didn't call again. Then he heard a noise—a small strange noise that could be a sobbing child.

"Cubby." He almost whispered the word. He didn't want to start those echoes again. "Where are you?"

"Here we are, Len."

Len couldn't tell from which direction the words came. They shattered around him, battering him from all sides. But the cat's pull on the belt was steady and in a minute he stumbled over the twins huddled on a pile of dried leaves. He dropped the belt which had brought him safely in as the twins flung themselves against him. Sobbing and crying, they clung to him as if they would never let him go.

"How did you get in here?" asked Len as soon as they were able to talk.

Cubby buried his face against Len's neck and cried harder than ever.

"We found your flashlight," explained Honey. "We wanted to see in the dark."

"Where is it?"

"It's lost again," wailed Cubby. "We lost it when we found the ghost."

"Ghost," gasped Len. "Where?"

"Don't be scared," said Honey. "It's just a kitty. Miss Nancy Rose's, I think, because she stayed with us a long time and we weren't afraid. She went away when we heard you and Glory."

"Oh." Len laughed in relief. "A cat."

"No. A kitten," said Honey. "The ghost is a kitten. I'm going to take it to Glory. It belongs to her because Miss Nancy Rose is her cat."

"We'll get it when we have a light," Len said, but he thought to himself if a kitten made the noise he and Glory had heard he didn't want to meet it in the dark. "Right now we're going home."

Holding their hands he turned, expecting to see the bright circle of light that marked the cave entrance. Instead there was only blackness, soft enfolding blackness.

He was puzzled. He knew he hadn't come far into the cave yet in that short distance he must have turned a corner. Around that corner would be the sun. But which way?

Keeping the twins well behind him he took two or three cautious steps. He bumped into the wall. Turning about he started the other way and again the wall blocked him.

Len was confused. He had lost all sense of direction. His better judgment told him to stay where he was. Glory would soon bring Papa and the other men who were at the cabin. He wouldn't have to wait long.

But his rising panic urged him to go on, to get the twins out of the cave as fast as he could. Hurry. Hurry. Only a few steps more and he would see again that bright circle of light.

Squeezing their hands until they hurt, he pulled the twins along. Suddenly the ground seemed to give way under their feet and they landed in a heap on the rocks below. Luckily the fall was not far and they were not hurt but it was enough to bring Len to his senses.

"What's the matter with you?" demanded Cubby. "The first thing you know you'll hurt Honey. Us men have to get her home."

Len began to laugh. He laughed because they were not hurt and because he was no longer afraid.

"The smart thing for us men to do is to sit tight where we are," he said. "I'll hold Honey until Papa comes."

"I think I made a mistake," and Cubby climbed into Len's lap. "I'm not as big as I thought I was. Hold me too."

They snuggled close and Len held them, laughing to himself as he leaned his head against Cubby's curls. It was only a minute or two until they were asleep. Len must have slept too for the next thing he knew a light was shining in his eyes and Papa was bending over him.

"Are you all right?" asked Papa. "Are they hurt?"

"They're only asleep," replied Len, blinking in the bright light.

He looked gratefully at the faces crowded about them. All the men from the cabin had come with Papa, each with a lantern or a flashlight. There were Sam Black and Jacob Miller, and Jed Taylor from the other side of Deer Knob. Behind a smoky coal oil lantern Len saw Grandpappy Bundie's toothless smile. There was even Lew Barnes who published the weekly paper at Lone Pine. He carried the biggest flashlight Len had ever seen.

"You too?" asked Len in surprise.

"I've got a nose for news," replied Mr. Barnes. "I came down for a story on Granny's new cabin and look what I ran into. What a headline. BIG BROTHER RESCUES SMALL CHILDREN FROM CAVE."

"Aw—it wasn't anything," said Len bashfully. "The cat led me right to them."

"A cat!" Mr. Barnes began to search for a pencil. "Your cat?"

"No. Glory's ghost cat." Len looked quickly at his father. "I mean—"

"I'm sure glad you got lost, young feller," interrupted Grandpappy Bundie. "I've always had a hankering to see this cave but I've been too scared to come. Now if you folks will just keep the boogers away I'd like to look around."

The men laughed and obligingly flashed their lanterns about the cave. Their laughter changed to exclamations of wonder and amazement. In the blaze of the lanterns the cave glowed with a thousand glittering lights. The walls glistened and the ceiling, sparkling with lights, was like the sky at night. Stalactites hung like fluted draperies from the roof. Stalagmites rose from the floor, delicate as spears of ice. They gleamed faintly pink, like clouds in the sunrise.

"What makes it shine?" asked Len in wonder. "Is it Spanish gold?"

"Probably bits of mica," replied Mr. Barnes. "Crystal reflects light, too. It could be that."

They all wandered about marveling at the beauty and the strangeness of the place. Len didn't even notice when Glory came in with the lantern from home.

"No wonder people thought this was a Spanish treasure cave," she said.

"The kind of treasure they couldn't carry away."

In the excitement Len forgot to tell her about Miss Nancy Rose's kitten.

13

Antiques for Sale

Don't take all that cream," warned Mamma. "That's all we have and Miss Nancy Rose hasn't had her breakfast."

Len grinned and tipped the pitcher to see if he dared take another spoonful. Papa winked at Glory.

"She takes the food right out of the mouths of her starving children to feed a stray cat," he said. "A bad luck cat, at that."

"Go along with you," said Mamma, stooping to scratch Miss Nancy Rose behind the ears. "She found the twins, didn't she? And you begrudge her a sip of cream. Nothing in the house is too good for this cat. Her's a sweet little kittsums, so her is."

Len groaned and rolled his eyes at Papa.

"Listen to her," he said. "Sweet little kittsums. It was only a day or two ago that she was yelling to get that pesky cat out of the house."

Mamma laughed, took the pitcher out of his hand and filled a bowl. Len snatched it as she set it back on the table. He squinted into the pitcher, then turned it up and squeezed the bottom. Not a drop came out.

Miss Nancy Rose had indeed moved into finer living quarters. Instead of the old cracked dish on the back porch, she now ate from a pretty red saucer that had come as a prize in a box of oatmeal. Her basket was lined with a sofa pillow—one of the best in the house. On the pillow in elegant comfort lay Echo, the kitten. Echo was exactly like her mother and although only one of her eyes was opened Glory was sure they would be blue.

"You young ones quit your giggling," said Mamma. "If you're going to buy a loom today we'd better be scurrying around."

They scurried and by nine o'clock they were on

the way to Oak Ridge. Len kept his hand in his pocket all the way. He was afraid one of those precious dimes would jiggle out.

A crowd had already gathered when they arrived. People milled about, peering into this, poking into that, quite as if they were at home. Glory knew some of them but most were strangers to her.

Furniture from the house was piled in the yard. Women lifted dishes to examine the marks on the underside. They exclaimed excitedly over broken chairs and tables. They pulled and picked at old quilts and coverlets. Glory couldn't understand why all the fuss over a lot of stuff that wasn't nearly as pretty as the furniture in the mail order catalogue.

Off to one side she found the loom. As far as she could tell it was a twin to the one Granny had used. She wanted to show Len but he and Papa had joined a crowd of men gathered around the farm tools.

The animals and tools were sold first. It was noon before the men wandered back to their families and the lunch baskets were opened. Some folks hadn't brought their own lunch. They bought food from a long table made of sawhorses and boards and covered with clean white tablecloths. The ladies from the church were selling pies, cakes and sandwiches to earn money for a new piano.

The auctioneer stood by, eating wedges of pie and drinking pop which was kept cold in a tub of ice. Glory watched him and when he wiped his mouth with the back of his hand she began shoving things into the basket.

"Hurry," she said. "He may begin with the loom."

Instead he began with an old marble top table. Glory was surprised at the amount of money a lady in a green hat paid for it. Several other articles were sold and she bit her finger nails in her bewilderment and anxiety.

She could see no reason for the prices. Really good things brought next to nothing while furniture, battered and scratched and older than your grandmother, brought an astonishing amount of money. By the time the auctioneer was ready to sell the loom both she and Len were depressed.

"There's no use even bidding," said Len hopelessly. "How far would nine dollars go?"

"It would start," replied Glory. "Maybe no one else will want it."

They elbowed their way to the front row as the auctioneer moved his box to the loom. Len had never bid at an auction before. He was shy and uneasy. Papa had told him to bid low at first to try out the crowd.

"Here's a fine old loom," began the auctioneer. "What am I bid?"

"One dollar." Len's voice squeaked in his excitement.

The crowd laughed and the auctioneer looked disgusted.

"This is a genuine antique. I've-got-a-dollar-but-I-want-more."

He talked so fast that his words all ran together. Glory could hardly understand him.

"Five dollars." That was from the woman in the green hat. Her tone said plainly she wasn't going to fool around with a little old dollar bid.

"I've got five. Who'll give me more?"

"Six." This from a woman in a red hat.

"Six-I've-got-six-I've-got."

"Seven," shouted Len. The bidding was getting away from him.

"Eight dollars." It was Green Hat again.

"Nine." Len and Red Hat shouted at the same time.

"Ten," said Green Hat.

"Twelve fifty," called Red Hat.

Len turned away and pushed through the crowd. Glory followed, her eyes so filled with tears that she bumped into the woman with the red hat.

"Excuse me, please," said Glory.

Papa was waiting for them at the edge of the crowd. The auctioneer's voice bellowed after them, still demanding more.

"Do you want to wait to see what it sells for?" asked Papa.

But neither Len nor Glory cared to. Red Hat and

Green Hat could fight it out without them. It didn't matter to them now what the loom brought.

The twins were asleep on a quilt in the back of the truck. Len and Glory climbed up beside them. It didn't seem possible that after all their work nine dollars could amount to so little.

"I didn't know so many people want to weave rugs," said Glory.

"I don't think they do, Glory," said Papa. "They probably want the loom to look at. It's an antique now."

"But Granny needs it," said Glory. "She could earn her living on it."

"I know it," Papa answered kindly. "But that's the way it is."

Glory was comforted a little to know that Papa was sorry too. Still it didn't change the fact that someone wanted the loom just to look at while Granny would have to go without the things she needed, like shoes and sugar, things her neighbors couldn't supply her with.

14

Honey Is Pretty Too

GLORY RAN to the window and pulled back the curtains. Rain was pouring from an overcast sky.

"Oh, no," she cried.

"What's the matter?" asked Cubby, sitting up in bed and rubbing the sleep from his eyes.

"It's raining. Len and I were going to town to get Granny's present. The party is tomorrow. Now look at it."

"Do you want me to help you cry?" asked Cubby obligingly.

"Silly. No," said Glory, laughing in spite of her ill humor. "You may as well get up but let Honey sleep."

"Honey might miss something if she sleeps," said Cubby. "We've got to get ready for the party too."

He put both feet in the middle of Honey's back and pushed. Honey rolled over and hit the floor with a bump. Cubby laughed. Honey raised up and bit his toe. Cubby grabbed her by the hair and shook. Honey bit harder.

"Mamma," screamed Cubby. "Honey's biting my toe."

"Stop that," said Glory crossly. She picked up a twin under each arm and set them on the floor—none too gently. "Isn't it enough that the day is spoiled without you two fighting?"

She left them making ugly faces and calling each other names while they struggled with their overalls. It didn't help her feelings any to have her mother exclaim over her long face when she went into the kitchen.

"We just have to get that present today and it's raining cats and dogs," she grumbled.

"It will fair up," said Mamma soothingly.

Honey Is Pretty Too

"Rain before seven
  Shine before eleven."

Glory didn't look quite so grumpy at that.

"Papa will take you," Mamma went on. "You and Len can choose the dishes without me. I'll stay and fix the lunch for tomorrow."

Mamma was right. By ten o'clock the rain had changed to a slow drizzle. Overhead there was enough blue sky to make a Dutchman a pair of britches so Glory knew that it wouldn't rain long. By the time she and Len climbed into the truck she had regained her good humor. They were still sorry about the loom but nine dollars would do nicely for a set of pretty dishes from the Five-and-Ten.

The twins watched them drive away. Then they wandered into the kitchen.

"What can we do, Mamma?" asked Cubby.

He leaned over Echo's basket but he didn't touch the kitten. Miss Nancy Rose was particular about her baby. Not everyone was permitted to touch her.

"There's an old magazine on the table," suggested Mamma. "Why don't you cut out pictures?"

"With the big scissors?" Honey asked hopefully.

"I guess so," replied Mamma, only half hearing

what Honey said as she measured sugar and flour for a cake.

The twins disappeared into the next room. Soon loud arguments of "That's mine" and "No, it's mine" told Mamma they were settled for some time to come.

She hurried about the kitchen. There was a lot to do this morning. The cake to finish, the chickens to fry, besides getting dinner. The folks planned to be back by noon.

The cake was cooling on the table and the black-eyed peas were sending tantalizing odors through the house when Mamma realized she hadn't heard the twins for some time. She hurried into the next room. The floor was covered with bits of paper but the twins weren't there.

"Cubby," she called.

"Here, Mamma." It was Honey who answered. "Cubby's making me pretty."

Mamma rushed into the bedroom but stopped in dismay at the door. On the floor sat Honey, her lap full of red curls. Heaped about her feet were tangled piles of red and yellow hair. Cubby's head was quite bare in spots, showing his clean pink scalp.

But not Honey's. Honey's straight locks were cov-

ered with dozens of red curls tied on with bits of
white string.

"I've got red curls too," she said, rolling her eyes
proudly up at her mother.

"Cubby!" cried Mamma. "What are you doing?"

"I'm making her pretty for the party," explained

123

Cubby. "Everyone says my hair is pretty. No one says her hair is pretty. I want her to be pretty like me."

"She was pretty to me," wailed Mamma.

Cubby didn't bother to answer. He tipped his head to one side and studied Honey's curls.

"This string is too long," he said. "I'll cut it off."

Waving the big scissors uncertainly he caught the string and snipped. The scissors snipped more than string. They took a bit of Honey's ear.

"Ouch," screamed Honey, clapping her hand to the side of her head. "Mamma, Cubby's cut off my ear."

Cubby dropped the scissors and threw his arms around her neck.

"Oh, Honey, don't cry. Please," he begged. "I didn't mean to hurt you. Let me kiss it."

He leaned over and looked inside her ear.

"Where does it hurt, my little Honey?" he asked tenderly.

Honey pointed to the tip of her ear. Cubby put a loud smack on the pink spot. He lifted her face and looked into her tear-filled eyes.

"Does it feel better now, my sweet little Honey?"

Honey nodded, sniffed and handed him another

red curl. Mamma picked up the scissors and hurried from the room. She bumped into Len and Glory who were just coming in, loaded with bundles.

"What's the matter, Mamma?" asked Len. "Are you sick?"

"Go look," she said, nodding toward the bedroom.

But the twins, strutting like turkey cocks, were close behind her. The red curls bobbed pertly as Honey tossed her head and smiled coyly behind the white strings that dangled in front of her eyes.

Len choked and covered his mouth but Glory didn't think it was anything to laugh at. She stared aghast at the haggled heads.

"Oh, Cubby, why did you do it?" she cried.

"To make her pretty like me," he answered, thrusting out his small chest.

"But couldn't you have tied your curls on her head without cutting her hair too?"

"Silly." Cubby looked at her, pitying her great ignorance. "Her head was already full of hair. I had to make room, didn't I?"

Len roared and Mamma laughed hysterically. Glory still couldn't see anything funny about it. The twins looked like mangy dogs and would look that way for weeks.

"Mamma," she demanded. "Aren't you going to punish them?"

"What for?" Mamma asked, wiping her eyes on her apron. "Punishment won't put the hair back."

"I declare." Glory slammed her bundles on the table. "Those kids get by with murder. How will they look at the party tomorrow?"

"Just like two young ones who have cut each other's hair," Mamma said. "Don't feel so bad about it, Glory. Set the table before Papa comes in."

Honey climbed into a chair and folded her hands.

"Papa will think I'm Cubby," she said.

Cubby climbed up beside her and folded his hands too.

"He'll never guess which is me and which isn't me," he chuckled.

Glory jerked open the cupboard door. The dishes clattered and banged as she slammed them on the table, all the while throwing angry glances at the giggling twins. Just when she wanted them to look their best they must make themselves ridiculous. Papa opened the door. The twins leaped from the chair and barged against him.

"Look. Look," Cubby shouted. "Isn't Honey pretty? See what I did?"

He danced about, yelling at the top of his voice, pushing Honey this way and that to show her curls to the best advantage.

Honey tried to talk but she couldn't stop Cubby long enough to make Papa hear. It wasn't right. She should be the one to tell Papa. They were her curls. She stepped up behind Cubby and put her hand over his mouth.

"See my red curls," she said grimly, holding Cubby, who kicked and struggled, by the nose.

"Well," said Papa, loosening her fingers, and Cubby gasped for breath. "Where did you get them?"

Honey smiled proudly at Cubby who was tenderly rubbing his pinched nose.

"He gave them to me," she said.

"I did not," yelled Cubby, pointing his finger at her. "She took them. She took those great big scissors and cut off every one of my curls."

Honey stared at him, surprised and hurt. Her mouth puckered and her chin began to tremble.

"He said I could have them," she explained as big tears spilled down her cheeks. "Papa, he told me to take them so I'd be pretty like him."

She leaned against Papa's knees and wept heart-

brokenly. Cubby watched her cry. He looked at
Mamma. She wasn't smiling now. Neither was Len
nor Glory. And Papa, who never scolded, was sorry
and ashamed. Cubby took a deep breath.

"I telled a lie," he said. "I telled Honey to take
them."

He walked over to the table. Little puffs of steam
were rising from the blackeyed peas. The corn bread
was just the way he liked it—yellow with brown
crust. His nose wiggled like a hungry puppy's. He
swallowed a couple of times, then he dragged his
chair to the corner and, climbing into it, he faced
the wall.

Honey watched him, her breath still coming in
long loud sobs. Suddenly she ran to the corner and
squeezed into the chair beside him. The red curls
and white strings trembled as she hid her face in
her hands. There was no sound except noisy sniffles.

"Mamma," whispered Len, grabbing his mother's
hand. "You aren't going to make them stay there."

"Tell them to get down," Glory begged. "Tell
them to eat with us."

Mamma looked at her in mild surprise.

"I thought you wanted them punished," she said.

"Not now I don't," Glory answered. "Please let them down."

"Five minutes is a long time to them," Mamma replied calmly. "Don't forget Cubby didn't tell the truth. They can sit there while I make the gravy."

The sniffles from the corner changed to noisy sobs. When Mamma turned to pour the gravy in the bowl, Len and Glory were perched on the chair with a twin on each lap.

15

Glory Buys a Loom

GLORY HAD NEVER known the scritch-scratch of Papa's razor to last so long. The pickup was already packed with the green table and the box of dishes. Papa's gift was a bale of hay for the cow. It wasn't exactly a housewarming gift but he said since Cindy was all the family Granny had she'd be proud to get the hay.

The twins looked mighty sweet in spite of their hair, Glory decided. Papa had smoothed up the ragged places with the clippers and now the thin spots were hardly noticeable.

Glory Buys a Loom

They sat on the steps clutching their gifts—glasses of apple jelly wrapped in white tissue paper—not daring to move for fear of spoiling their new clothes. Honey's flowered dress was made from a feed sack. So was Cubby's shirt, but Papa had bought his overalls yesterday while Glory and Len selected Granny's dishes.

"I declare, Glory, you make me nervous." Mamma was flustered and impatient as she rushed about putting last things in the lunch basket. "Put Echo outside where Miss Nancy Rose can take care of her. Then you go on down by the trail. We'll have to go the long way around by the road."

Glory set the basket on the porch where it would be protected from the wind. The cat licked Glory's hand. For a while after Echo came Miss Nancy Rose was too busy being a mother to bother with such things as petting or playing with Glory. But now that the kitten was able to tumble about on spraddling unsteady legs, she turned again to Glory.

"Take care of your baby while I'm gone."

Miss Nancy Rose clung to Glory and tucked her head under her chin—a gesture Glory loved. It made her think of the long walk home from the haunted house with the forlorn cat sleeping trustfully in her arms.

Again came that nagging thought. The cat really didn't belong to her. Suppose she wasn't an abandoned cat, unwanted, left to hunt her own way or starve. Suppose instead she was lost and someone was mourning for her now as Glory would mourn if she had to give her up. Glory put the unpleasant thought out of her mind. She placed the cat in the basket and hurried along the trail.

So many folks had planned to come to Granny's housewarming that the party had turned into a picnic in Witch Hollow. Word had got around of the wonders of Witch Cave and folks were anxious to see for themselves. Len had gone to the cave early with Mr. Barnes. They wanted the lanterns lighted and in place when the crowd came.

Glory glanced at the sky. No rain today and that was good. She walked slowly down the stone stairway, watching the people who had already come. Two men were measuring off the distance for the horseshoe toss. A fire was burning in the old fireplace. Later there would be roasted wieners and hamburgers. Already the pool was crowded with boys and girls, early as it was.

In the cave she found Grandpappy Bundie with Mr. Barnes and Len. Mr. Barnes' powerful light was focused on a hole in the wall at which they were staring in excitement.

"Listen, Glory," said Len. "Do you recognize that noise?"

A moan, rising, falling, rising again—so faint Glory had to strain her ears to hear—whispered through the cave.

"That's it, Len. That's the noise we heard. Only it was a thousand times louder."

Grandpappy Bundie looked as if he might start running at any minute.

"That's it! I'd know that screechin' at the pearly gates. What is it?"

"The wind," answered Mr. Barnes. "It's my opinion there's another cave beyond this one. That small opening has an outside entrance somewhere and the wind, when it's in a certain direction, whistles through it. What do you say we explore that cave some time?"

"How?"

"We'll make the hole big enough to crawl through. Are you coming too, Grandpappy?"

"By cracky, I will," laughed Grandpappy. "Now that I know the boogers won't get me."

Glory grinned knowingly at Len.

"Are you afraid of the boogers?"

"I'm cured too," he said. "I'm raring to go."

"Hey, Len. Can we come in?"

Bud Miller with a crowd of boys was peering in the entrance.

"Sure. Come on."

Glory left the cave and went up to the cabin. The room was so filled with people that she could hardly see the gifts which they had brought. It was like a dozen Christmases rolled into one. Mamma was there setting out the new dishes and proudly telling everyone that her young ones had earned the money to buy them.

Glory squeezed herself into a corner and watched Granny's friends come and go. She understood now what Granny had meant when she said "Folks around here are bound together in friendship." Friendship brought people together to work for a common cause. Friendship had built a house and furnished it.

There were curtains made from gaily flowered feed sacks at the windows. There were quilts on the

bed and food on the shelves. The room was almost as pretty as it had been before the fire.

Only one thing was missing. The corner where the loom should have stood was empty. Glory slipped away. The dishes were pretty and Granny was proud of them but they couldn't bring in the extra money that she needed. Glory went back to the grove hoping that by this time some of the girls she played with at school would be there.

Late in the afternoon Glory noticed a crowd of boys gathered at the entrance of the cave. Suddenly they began to shout and a shower of rocks whizzed through the air. A flash of white raced along the ledge and disappeared up a tree. Glory dashed across the creek and pushed her way through the crowd.

"That's my cat you're throwing at," she cried angrily. "Don't you dare touch her."

Some of the boys dropped the rocks but Bill Warner sent his stone sailing into the tree where the cat crouched against a limb.

"Aw—smarty," he shouted. Reaching out, he jerked off one of her hair ribbons. "What are you going to do about it?"

"Just this," said Glory.

She lunged at Bill and pushed with all her might. There was a mighty splash as Bill toppled backwards into the water.

"If that doesn't teach you to let my cat alone I'll call Len," she cried, glaring around at the other boys.

"Let her alone," cautioned Bud, looking hastily around for Len. "The cat's not hurting anyone."

The boys vanished into the cave while Bill climbed sullenly out of the water.

It was sometime before Glory could coax Miss Nancy Rose from the tree. Her eyes were wild with fright when she finally backed down to where Glory could reach her. Glory carried her to a log by the side of the road. There, away from the noise and the crowd, the cat stopped trembling and lay quietly on Glory's lap.

"She's a beautiful cat, isn't she?"

Glory looked up in surprise. Beside her was a woman in a red hat who was gazing in delight at Miss Nancy Rose. Glory recognized her as the woman who had bid on the loom at the sale.

"I think she's beautiful," Glory said shyly. "The most beautiful cat in the world."

"You aren't far wrong," replied the woman. "May I touch her?"

The woman held out her hand and Miss Nancy Rose sniffed her fingers. To Glory's surprise she even gave them a quick lick but she turned quickly and snuggled her head under Glory's chin. A look of disappointment passed over the woman's face.

"She's not used to strangers," explained Glory. "I'm surprised she licked your fingers."

The woman studied Miss Nancy Rose a long time, so long that Glory began to feel uneasy.

"I'm Mrs. Brent," said the woman at last. "I raise white Persian cats. Maybe you've heard of them. They've taken blue ribbons at cat shows all over the country."

"You mean first prize like the blue ribbons at the fair?" asked Glory. "I didn't know there were shows for cats."

"Yes, there are," said Mrs. Brent. "Would you like to sell your cat?"

"Oh, no," said Glory. "I couldn't. I love her and she loves me. Don't you, Miss Nancy Rose."

"Miss Nancy Rose," said Mrs. Brent. "What an odd name for a cat. How did you happen to call her that?"

Glory Buys a Loom

Glory told of finding the cat, half starved, at the old haunted house. She repeated the story of the real Nancy Rose who had once lived there.

"The cat had a blue ribbon around her neck when I found her," she explained. "There didn't seem to be any other name for her. My brother calls her a ghost cat when my father isn't around."

"Didn't I see you and your brother at the sale?"

"Yes," said Glory. "We bid on the loom."

"Do you weave rugs?"

"No," answered Glory. "We didn't want it for ourselves. We wanted it for Granny."

"Tell me about Granny."

Mrs. Brent's voice was kind. She smoothed the cat's thick ruff while Glory told about the fire and how Granny needed the loom to make money because her friends were unable to pay cash for her work.

"Len and I sold berries but we didn't earn enough," she finished.

"Do you still want the loom?" asked Mrs. Brent.

"Yes, but we don't have any money now. We bought new dishes with our nine dollars."

Mrs. Brent said nothing for some time. Glory

wished she would go away. There was something disturbing about this woman.

"Anyway," said Glory, hoping to close the conversation, "I don't know where the loom is. We didn't wait to see who bought it."

"I bought it," replied Mrs. Brent. "It's out in the trailer of my car, the one parked there against the hill. I have an antique shop in Tulsa. Several times a year I drive through this part of the country looking for old furniture. I come to picnics like this because often I meet people who have things to sell. But as I told you, I also raise white Persian cats. I'll give you the loom if you will give me your cat."

"No. No," cried Glory. She was angry but she didn't know why. She only knew that she wanted Mrs. Brent to go away and never come back. "No. I won't trade Miss Nancy Rose for all the looms in the world."

She closed her eyes to shut out the sight of that hateful red hat. Miss Nancy Rose snuggled closer. Her sharp claws dug into Glory's shoulders but they didn't hurt as much as this terrible thing Mrs. Brent had suggested.

She could hear the folks laughing in Witch Hollow—Granny's friends, laughing because Granny was happy again, happy because of a new house all furnished. All furnished except for a loom.

"I couldn't." There was a catch in Glory's voice. "I couldn't give my cat away."

Granny's face, wrinkled and kind, rose before her. Granny, hurrying along the trail with her basket of healing medicines. Granny removing a splinter from Glory's finger once a long time ago, talking all the while so she wouldn't mind the pain. Granny on her knees before Len, his foot all swollen and red from a rusty nail. Granny, leaning over the twins' bed last winter when they were so sick with the measles they didn't know anybody, not even Mamma and Papa.

The pictures crowded through her mind. There were Granny's old shoes drying on the oven door, wet through because she had no overshoes. Granny in her stocking feet because her only shoes were wet.

Granny? Miss Nancy Rose? Granny?

Glory rubbed her cheek against Miss Nancy Rose's head. She felt the sharp tickle of the long

141

silvery whiskers. Leaning down she kissed the cat between her delicately pointed ears.

"Take her," Glory said. "Tell my father to put the loom by the window."

Glory turned and ran swiftly toward home.

16

Echo Makes a Choice

GLORY DROPPED down on the steps. She was glad there was nobody at home. She would have a little time before she had to talk. A little time in which to get used to the idea of being without Miss Nancy Rose.

She wished she could forget that last frightened cry as she had put the cat in Mrs. Brent's arms. It kept beating into her ears. Miss Nancy Rose would think Glory had deserted her. And she had. She had given her away. There was a thump, a small cry, and Echo scrambled into Glory's lap.

143

Echo. Glory had forgotten all about Echo. The kitten cried. She was hungry. She wanted her mother.

"Oh, Echo," Glory said. The tears she had held back so long began to fall. "You're hungry and I've given away your mother."

She carried Echo into the house and poured some milk into a saucer. Lighting a lamp she held the saucer over the flame so the milk would heat. Then she set the dish on the floor.

Echo would have none of it. She didn't know how to drink from a dish. Glory dipped her finger into the milk and put a drop on the kitten's tongue but Echo continued to cry. Glory was still trying to get Echo to drink when Mamma opened the door.

"Oh, Mamma!" she cried. "I've done something terrible."

"No, you've done something fine," said Mamma.

"But Echo. She's hungry. I forgot about her," sobbed Glory.

Her mother rummaged through a drawer and found an old medicine dropper. She washed it and heated the milk again. Then drop by drop she fed Echo. It took a long time but at last the crying stopped. While the kitten slept on her lap, Mamma told Glory how happy Granny had been when the loom was carried into her house.

"Everyone thought you were right smart to make such a fine trade with Mrs. Brent," said Mamma proudly but Glory wasn't sure.

"Did Papa put it in the corner by the window?" she asked listlessly.

She didn't care just now where he had put the loom but she had to say something. Even Mamma must not know how bad she felt.

"I didn't wait to find out," replied her mother. "When I heard what you had done, I came home by the trail. I figured you might be having trouble with the kitten."

Glory smoothed the kitten's button-like nose with one finger. She was glad her mother had come early. At least Echo was happy.

Nothing was said about the cat when the rest of the family came home. Even the twins were quiet when Glory pushed her chair away from the supper table, leaving her food untouched.

When bedtime came, Glory put Echo's basket beside her bed. She covered it with a light blanket to keep the kitten warm. Several times during the night when Echo cried she heated milk over the flame of the lamp and fed the kitten.

Glory was still tired when she heard the twins chattering the next morning. They sounded more excited than usual but she didn't open her eyes. They were always excited about something. It wouldn't be worth while getting up to see what caused it. She wanted to go back to sleep. She didn't want to face the long lonely day that was before her.

She turned over and felt the familiar warmth of soft fur, the comforting pressure of a small head beneath her chin. Glory lifted her hands slowly, fearful that this might be another dream. But the rough tongue against her cheek, the needle-sharp claws kneading her shoulder were no dream.

"Mamma," she screamed. "Mamma."

Not only her mother but the rest of the family rushed into the room, the twins pushing and crowding to reach the bed first. They all began to talk at once. Finally Glory understood that when Mamma opened the door this morning Miss Nancy Rose had walked in.

"I declare to goodness," said Mamma. "She's the strangest cat I ever saw. She rushed right past her own baby to jump up beside you. I had to lift her down to make her feed Echo. She's been snuggled against you for the last hour."

Glory hid her face against the pillow.

"She's not mine any more," she said miserably. "I gave her away."

"Don't worry," said Papa. "I went down to Lone Pine this morning and saw M⸱ s. Brent. She's coming to see you."

"You'd better dress," said her mother. "She'll be here before long."

Mamma laid out a clean dress. Glory saw that it was the pink one with lace that she wore to Sunday school. Usually she loved to wear the dress but today she wished it could be her oldest, most patched and faded dress. Then she could hand Miss Nancy Rose once more to Mrs. Brent and she could run away into the woods and stay there until this terrible lump went out of her throat.

"I'll brush your hair," said Mamma, taking the brush from Glory's cold hands. "You'll want to look your best."

Glory didn't care whether she looked her best or not. The price she had paid for Granny's loom was growing dearer by the minute. She hadn't known it would be so hard. She hadn't counted on having to give Miss Nancy Rose away twice.

"Now don't worry," said Mamma, giving Glory's pink bow a final pat as a knock sounded on the door.

Glory sat uneasily on the edge of her chair while Papa and Mamma made Mrs. Brent welcome. They gave her the best chair, placed where she could feel the cool morning breeze. They talked about the weather and the mountains, about everything but cats.

Glory knew that all these things must be said. The guest must not be made to feel hurried or unwanted but it was hard to sit calmly when she knew that Miss Nancy Rose was crouched under the bed in the farthest corner of the bedroom, fearful that she should be carried away again.

"Mrs. Brent," Papa said at last. "My wife and I have been talking things over since I saw you this morning. It seems that our girl and the cat kind of belong together. If you could give us a little time we think we could pay for the loom."

He smiled at Glory's amazed face.

"Of course," he went on, "we couldn't pay you all at once. A dollar or two at a time is the best we could do."

"I'll pick berries as long as they last," broke in Len, "and send you the money."

"We'll all help," said Mamma. "I think I could sell a few loaves of home-baked bread down at Lone Pine. Some cookies too, maybe. Tourists like such things I hear when they're on vacation."

"It isn't as serious as all that," protested Mrs. Brent. "The loom didn't cost enough—"

Just then Echo scampered into the room. She bounced across the floor like a windblown snow-flake, her eyes bright as shiny blue beads. Sidling up to Mrs. Brent she sniffed her shoes, then dug her claws into her skirt. Mrs. Brent lifted the kitten to her lap.

Echo shut her eyes and tried to purr. It was a choking bubbling noise. Still, without a doubt, it was meant to be a purr. Cubby walked over and leaned down to listen.

"You know something," he said seriously. "Echo is a newer model than Miss Nancy Rose and I think she has a bigger motor. Listen to her."

"And do you know something," said Mrs. Brent with a laugh. "I think I like the new model best. At least she likes me. Glory, when Echo is big enough to leave her mother, will you give her instead of her

149

mother to me? If you will I'll consider the loom paid for."

"A kitten for a loom?" protested Papa.

"Don't forget I raise Persian cats," replied Mrs. Brent. "She will be worth more than the loom to me. I know where Miss Nancy Rose came from. Glory, the owner will never want your cat again. What do you say? May I have Echo?"

Glory opened her mouth but before she could answer a streak of white dashed across the room. With noisy excited cat-talk Miss Nancy Rose settled herself on Glory's lap and glared defiantly at the amazed faces around her. She spoke one last convincing "Meow," laid her head on Glory's knee and shut her eyes.

"That, I take it, is my answer," said Mrs. Brent.

"Would you believe it?" said Papa. "She knows she's safe."

"Why shouldn't she know?" said Len with a wink at Glory and a sidelong glance at his father. "She's not a real cat. She's a—"

He caught his father's stern frown and stopped.

Glory held the cat close. The tight ache in her heart was gone. Miss Nancy Rose was her own— her very own little ghost cat—to keep forever and ever.